Love Gaia
~ The Diary Directive

By TL Clark

Published in the United Kingdom by:

Steamy Kettle Publishing

First published in electronic format and in print in 2020.

ISBN: 978-0-9956117-5-7

Acknowledgements

Cover design by Robin Ludwig Design Inc.

www.gobookcoverdesign.com

The image of the rabbit on the cover was actually created by www.tattootribes.com

- It incorporates specific, meaningful Maori symbols

My alpha, beta, proof and ARC readers – I can't thank you and my editor enough. Your support is deeply appreciated.

Thanks also to Hubby. He's always supportive, but the final edits of this book were carried out during the COVID-19 lockdown. Thank you so much for your extra patience and quiet space to do what this book demanded. I love you to the moon and back.

And last but by no means least, thank you, dear reader, for giving my book a happy home. I hope you enjoy reading this as much as I enjoyed writing it.

Chapter 1

Aroha tugged at the long sleeves of her white robes, pulling them further over her wrists.

"Mum, explain to me again why we have to walk all that way outside to the diary house in the heat," she whined in the mild Kiwi accent of their race.

Rolling her dark brown eyes and heaving a deep sigh, her mum repeated the words she'd uttered several times on the run-up to this momentous day, "Sweetheart, all will become clear once you have begun this journey. Your brief suffering is nothing compared to that of our ancestors. It is our way of honouring their journey."

Checking her daughter's white gloves were well tucked under her sleeves so no skin was bared to the harsh midday sun, she took a step back.

"Oh, my darling, you are so grown up," she said, wiping a tear away.

Now that Aroha was judged to have reached maturity, she was worthy of receiving the full details of their past. It was an edict passed down through the generations, lest they forget the mistakes of their ancestors.

The large, circular, white sunhat kept the girl's face shaded. Her long, black hair was coiled on top of her head, hidden from view. The high neck of the hemp robes ensured maximum UV protection was achieved. Despite having brown skin, Aroha was not immune to the harsh rays.

1

Three knocks rapped on their door.

"It is time," her mum announced as if Aroha had not heard the signal herself.

With a quick hug, she ushered her daughter out the door where she joined a line of similarly attired boys and girls, all ready to attend today's lesson. It marked an important part of their journey to adulthood.

Proud parents formed their own lines behind their offspring until they reached the atrium. Sobbing and cheering could be heard in equal measure, along with clapping and chatting as the young adults congregated. But all were silenced by the clang of a gong.

Only the shuffling of feet on the sand floor was audible as the teenagers ensured their correct places were taken.

The gong resounded with a second strike. With heads bowed and hands clasped in front, the white figures began filtering outside. Aroha's mum's hand flew to her chest. Ordinarily, nobody would dare go out at this time of day. Worry mixed with pride in her bosom as her daughter embarked on her voyage.

The parents remained behind, huddled in the meeting house where they could reassure and comfort one other until their young returned.

Meanwhile, the teenagers walked in subdued silence.

Sweat beaded on every brow as the procession made its long, steep way to the diary house; the most sacred building in Fort Itude. Nestled on the edge of the cliffs, it overlooked the sea.

The sweet, salty smell drifted across the group. All attendees breathed deeply, savouring the fresh scent. The cool breeze coming off that watery expanse was a welcome reprieve.

The reading mistress, Rongo, led them into the reading house, her peach skin barely visible underneath her own robes. Quietly, they each found a floor cushion to sit on. Nobody dared utter a sound. Many stared at the writing on the wall, focussing on their motto, "**Honesty, Respect, Fortitude**". The black, swirling form of a rabbit sat above it.

A jug of water was passed around, along with cups so the class could recover from the arduous journey.

Once they were all settled, Rongo lit the white candle in its jar. The illumination briefly highlighted her espresso eyes. Released from the confines of her hat now they were indoors, her tawny hair cascaded to her shoulders.

Spreading her arms wide, she announced, "Let us give our thanks to the ancestors."

"Thanks be to them," was echoed around the room by the young attendees.

"May we live by their wisdom," Rongo chanted.

"May we honour them."

"And may we cherish our beloved planet, Gaia."

Bowing forwards, their hands on the floor, the attendants intoned, "Love to Gaia."

Rongo repeated their action and words. As they all sat upright, they observed meditative silence for a few minutes.

On a wooden rest in front of Rongo was a copy of the diary, their treasured text she was to read from. A rabbit was depicted on the closed cover.

Looking up at the eager faces, she stated, "We are here today to begin the lessons of our truth. You have been declared ready to hear our history so you may better build our future."

"We will listen," they chanted.

Reverently, Rongo turned to the first page and began to read out loud.

*"This book belongs to Dr. Rachel Rose. I belong to **The Diary Directive**, a group formed at the emergency meeting in South Africa, 2069 to record the truth of this situation.*

We each pledge to be honest and record matters of importance as they occur in our own notebooks. What may yet be, we can only guess. But of this we are certain:

THIS IS ALL OUR FAULT!

Humans are about to destroy the world. And they are already lying about it.

This is why we agreed to record our lives, however long or short they may be.

My wish for you, whoever you are, is this:

That you contain HONESTY in your heart,

RESPECT in every thought and action,

and FORTITUDE to see you through.

Entry 1 – 12th March 2069

I was flown here from Liverpool, England to somewhere in South Africa to attend a crisis counsel. Informed only that my expert medical opinion was urgently required, I was driven to the airport without being permitted to explain my departure to my family. My trust is in a government agent who remained at my house and said she would relay all relevant information but as time was of the essence, I was to leave there and then.

Having watched enough spy films in my youth, I would be foolish to trust these people. But they accepted no questions or opposition. I was all but frog-marched at gunpoint. Suspecting they concealed weapons under their suits, I thought it best not to argue yet feared for my life.

Please let my husband and children be safe. Tears fall as I write this now. I didn't even say goodbye.

(return after a pause) I must carry on. This is now my solemn duty.

I arrived here with many other doctors, nurses, consultants and surgeons from all over the globe. All looked as confused and concerned as me as we were herded into the auditorium. The venue seems to be an abandoned zoo. A curious location which does nothing for my anxiety. It's eerie in its empty state.

There were three speakers at the meeting, two men and one woman. They took it in turns to alert us to "the meteor which is about to hit Earth". Emergency evacuation is underway, and we are part of it. We are to be flown to one of several secret locations where we will be housed safely for the good and future of the human race.

Meteor, my arse. It is no secret that war has been building. First, the bees died out, killed by our pesticides is the common belief, although they tried to conceal even this. Crops failed year after year without their pollination; food grew ever more scarce. Famine - a global famine descended.

Land with any viable growth became ever more sought after. With an over-populated, hungry world, anger flared like a furnace. First came the riots. Then skirmishes. Local battles broke out. Things had been steadily escalating. So much anger and ferocity!

And now, although I never would have believed it, I fear some global powers, our governments and leaders are about to launch nuclear weapons. Idiots!

What purpose is there in fighting for polluted land? We have so few resources left. This will only make it worse.

I digress. We were permitted a lunch break. A small group of us were seated together, having spoken briefly over morning coffee. Coffee; what a joke. These people still have some, having obviously hoarded the stuff or even managing to grow it somewhere. And they act as if it were normal.

Tentatively, in a whisper, I hint at my suspicions to the people sitting with me. Not one of us disagreed. We are educated people with inquisitive minds. Rumours have spread to America, Russia, India and China, given the nationalities, information and places of work of my friends. Yes, friends. I have to trust these people. We have been thrown together.

A few were momentarily curious about my accent; apparently, they'd not heard "northern English" before. My Scouse accent means words like proper sound like propehh, and up is more uhp... this was initially a shock for my new friends, but we couldn't dwell on it for long. Besides, we could all understand one another and have greater concerns.

Constantly watched, we walked away from the canteen after our substantial meal. I have not seen so much food in months. Yes, they have prepared.

Our group walked along to what was once a gift shop and ducked under the not-quite-closed shutters.

The shelves were still fully stocked. How long ago did people leave this place? And how suddenly were they driven out? Chills run through me at the thought. At least there was no sign of blood. But neither were there any signs of life; even the cages lay vacant.

We each picked up a few notebooks and pens in the gift shop, secreting them in our clothes and bags. I had no cash to leave in exchange. It's not like I had the chance to pop to the Bureau de Change. Maybe I've stolen these items? Maybe nobody will ever return here – if so, is that still theft?

Moral dilemmas aside, we thought it funny how mine have a rabbit on the front and the nurse from China choose ones with pandas. I don't wish to detail too much for fear of getting them into trouble if this diary's ever discovered.

We walked out, empty water bottles in our arms, trying to throw the military security off the scent. It worked. The officers we soon encountered told us to put the bottles down. We put up an argument that they may prove useful, but they were adamant that everything we need will be provided.

Making a show of being disappointed, we begrudgingly put the bottles on the floor. Fortunately, everyone was called back into the auditorium, so we were hurried along without being searched.

The speakers then told us we were to be issued with medical kits to take with us, and then directed to planes.

In order to be ready to hit the ground running, we were to immediately change into the scrubs provided. In shock, we all filed into queues, accepting the items with open arms.

They must have been expecting their meteor at any moment.

Feigning a loo break, I took my new belongings into the toilets. Ripping open the bottom of my newly issued bag, I quickly shoved the stolen books and pens inside, careful to time my actions with loo flushes from the other cubicles.

My mobile phone had already been taken from me as soon as I got in the car at home, otherwise that would have gone in too.

Following the crowds, I went into the female changing area and complied. There have been too many occurrences of this type of behaviour in history where people do not return. My limbs quivered so much it was a challenge to get dressed at all.

Our own clothes were taken away. Army soldiers guided us to vehicles which would take us to the airport. At this point, I could only hope that part was true. The alternative was that we were being led to our death, and that was too much to even think about.

Boarding the aircraft with an element of relief, I strapped myself into the seat. According to the announcement on the plane, we've been flown to New Zealand. My fellow passengers weren't just medical staff from the conversations I heard.

We were sent on different aircraft to avoid losing all of us in the event of an accident; not a terribly comforting thought, but at least they seemed concerned over our safety. Plus, we wouldn't all have fitted on one.

I've already been divided from the friends I made at the zoo. I hope they're OK.

It is clear this is a large scale evacuation, larger even than they inferred in their fine speech.

After a long, anxious flight and with eerie military precision, we were all directed to our quarters to await further instruction. And so I wait."

Rongo paused, looking up at open-mouthed faces.

The story was more riveting than the worst horror folk tales her students had heard so far in the young lives.

Of course, they had heard roughly of the tales of their beginnings, but this was in full detail. No softening so as not to scare children now.

The fear leapt off the pages, tremored in Rongo's own voice as she spoke. Tears were falling from several pairs of eyes, and this was just the start.

Chapter 2

Aroha could hardly believe what she was hearing. She was too stunned to ask her many questions when the reading mistress asked if anyone had any.

"Where's England, Rongo?" one boy asked, a frown above his now dark but usually twinkling brown eyes.

"Remember how the lands were all given names in the Before?" she answered, fetching the cherished atlas.

Finding the right page, she held it up for the group to see. "This is us, what they used to call New Zealand," she said, pointing, "And right up here was England."

"But it's so far away. How did she get here? She said something about a plane?"

"Gerald, we studied planes when we looked at history. They used to have giant metal tubes with wings which could climb up into the sky," Hana informed him, flicking her chestnut hair away from her hazel eyes.

"I know, but so far? I just don't see how they could do it."

"Well, we know they could even if we're not sure how. Dr. Rachel said so herself in this diary," Rongo gently pointed out.

"But why did she not believe her leaders?" Hana asked without raising her hand.

"I know it's hard to understand. But humans are capable of deep deception. We know they used to lie lots and how badly they were punished for it. That's why it's so important to always be honest now. It's in our tribal motto to remind us. Back then, I think maybe people felt bad about what they'd done and didn't want to admit it. Like if you break something and are worried your parents will be angry with you."

The girl scrunched her tan nose and winced underneath her long, dark fringe. "Hmm, I guess so. But then I tell mum or dad and we discuss what was bad and I never do it again."

"That's a very good point, Hana. When we talk about our mistakes we learn, don't we?"

A lot of heads nodded at Rongo.

"They were yet to learn."

"They were stupid and bad," Hana stated firmly.

"They were certainly wrong. But we must be careful when labelling others as good, bad or stupid. As we continue, we'll learn more about how terrible things happen when we lie. Are we all ready to continue?"

More head nods were her cue to go on with the reading.

"13th March 2069

I was called to a meeting for the medics, and I'm more confused than ever. And tired. Jet lag is affecting me and maybe the trauma of the last twenty-four hours is impacting my mental health. I wrote in a hurry yesterday. Words tumbled out.

I didn't even describe where I am; a terrible oversight. There were some locals present at the meeting, including some Maori. I couldn't help but mentally cheer the tiny effort at diversity. But they have confirmed we are in caves outside Hamilton, New Zealand. It's such a pity it was dark when we landed. I slept for a lot of the coach trip from the airport. I suspect we were given sleeping drafts in our drinks on board the plane as nobody seems to have stayed awake. Given the high levels of anxiety, this is very strange.

We are deep underground, supposedly safe from said meteor. At least they're consistent with the story. Maybe, by sheer coincidence, a meteor **is** bound for Earth. I don't know. All my colleagues seem to share my misgivings, not that we're permitted much time to talk and are still observed every minute.

I feel strange. My head is foggy. My words won't seem to behave on the page. There is so much I want to tell you but find myself unequal to the task. Perhaps it is best that I rest now and try again tomorrow. It feels important that what I write here is clear.

14th March 2069

Two days I have been down here, and we're not allowed to go up to the surface. More people arrived yesterday evening. Nobody can tell us how long we're to be kept here. Nothing's happening. I'm used to a constant stream of patients. I work in the oncology unit at the Alder Hey Children's Hospital in Liverpool. Or did. So far, there are no major emergencies to deal with. We have all been carefully selected, so are in good health. I've not even seen any children here yet.

And there's the thing. Why would they need a cancer specialist after an asteroid hit? Emergency room doctors and nurses are present, which is sound. But what am I here for?

Nervous anticipation buzzes through our groups when we gather. We all seem to be waiting. What for? We don't really know. But it feels ominous. The calm before the storm.

Nobody has a phone. I have no way of contacting home. I ache for my family. Are they safe? Why couldn't they come with me? It's cruel. Joshua is six and Ella is four. How they must be missing their mummy. And how I miss them and their daddy, Theo. Will I ever see them again? Oh my God, I'm going to go crazy. If only they'd let me phone them. I just want to hear their voices, know they're alright."

Sobs could be heard from Rongo's audience. She had to wipe away tears from her own cheeks. No matter how many times she read this, she could never get over the cruelty of breaking up families. And not to even be able to say goodbye. Who were these barbarians? How did they ever think they were saving humanity when they clearly had none themselves?

"I think that's enough for today. Let's get you back to your own parents. I'm sure you need to see them now."

More eager nods answered her and some brave people managed to vocalise a, "Yes, please."

They walked back down the hill to the meeting house, arm-in-arm. Rongo didn't hush them; they needed each other's compassionate words now. There was no easy way to teach this. The truth can be painful, but that's no reason to shy away from it. Knowledge is vital. Humans must never again stray down that dark path.

The teenagers ran into their parents' open arms as soon as they saw them in the atrium. Many bursting into tears again. Many hands stroked hair released from hats, kisses were planted on cheeks and plenty of hugs were issued.

"Come, we have a special meal planned for this evening. There's cider," Rongo announced, clearly trying to sound cheerful but not quite succeeding.

"Mum, it's so sad. Dr. Rachel was taken from her home and brought here alone without her family," Aroha said into her mother's neck as she held her.

"I know, sweetheart, I know. But that's never going to happen to you. You have me and Dad. We're here."

With that, her dad managed to push through the crowd and joined the cuddle. Aroha clung on with all her might. The thought of being separated from either of them brought more tears from her eyes.

"We remember them," her mum said.

"Yes, we remember. Oh, mum, I don't want to go back. I don't want to hear any more."

"We can talk about it later. Let's go and have some food for now. See how you feel later, eh?"

"I'm not sure I can eat."

Her dad interjected, "Now, Aroha, we can't be wasteful. Dr. Rachel wouldn't like us to be unappreciative, would she?"

"No, dad. I'm sorry."

"Hush, no need for sorries. Let us say a prayer for her this mealtime. Give extra thanks."

"Yes, yes, I'd like that."

They went to the smaller dining hall attached to the meeting house. This evening was a special event for the new adults. Sweet treats and comfort food had been specially prepared. The first day was always the hardest.

After the normal prayers of gratitude were over, Aroha's dad stood from the table.

"Everyone, I hope it's OK. We'd like to add an additional prayer today."

"But, of course, go ahead," Rongo agreed.

All heads bowed again. "Dear Source, we thank you for the gift of Dr. Rachel Rose, for her bravery and sacrifice. Thank you for delivering her diary unto us. May we always remember the lessons and live with honesty, respect and fortitude."

"Honesty, Respect, Fortitude," they all chorused.

A great clattering resounded as they all began to tuck into their feast. Most of the time, they were very responsible with the amount of food they consumed, never taking more than they gave to the land. But special days called for a lapse in the rules. And make no mistake, embarking on this intense history lesson was to be celebrated.

One of their founders, Dr. Rachel Rose was the start of their civilisation. They were alive because of her and her subsequent followers. Thanks be to them.

Chapter 3

The next morning, Aroha was less nervous about her behaviour as they congregated but more apprehensive over what she may hear. Yesterday had been every bit as hard as she'd been warned it would be. And the story could only get worse. No, not a story. The memoir; this all really happened. That is what made it so awful.

With deep breaths, Aroha joined her fellow students for their pilgrimage to the reading house. The ritual was the same every day; the long, hard, hot walk followed by meditation to candlelight and offering thanks.

"Does anyone have any questions before we begin today?" Rongo checked.

All heads shook their no.

"Are you sure? You can ask anything. This is a safe place. And I need to know you're OK."

Head nods indicated the students were sure. Rongo understood that they were too nervous to express themselves right now.

"Alright then. But stop me if you need to."

"I will," echoed around in promise.

"So, where were we? Dr. Rachel was brought to our land, having been separated from her family and she was worried about them more than her own safety. She was in a cave, not yet sure of her purpose."

"15th March 2069

Today, we were allowed a little more communal time. First, we were brought out of our rooms and marched down to a great hall. I recognised one of the speakers from the initial crisis meeting in South Africa, but the others were new to me. They informed us that the meteor is likely to strike soon now. I wish I could trust them, believe this isn't all an almighty cover-up. But my conscience keeps warning me otherwise.

The speakers left the stage and we took the opportunity to talk, observed, of course. The bloke on my right is also my neighbour accommodation-wise. His name is Mike and he has kind, blue eyes and short, dark blond hair. His skin is almost as pale as mine. He also came from England and was a top surgeon at Great Ormond Street Hospital in London. It's oddly comforting to meet someone with similar hair and eye colour to mine.

We were both ruminating over the requirement for child specialists when no children are present, but then the person on my left spoke up.

She's a stunningly beautiful lady, named Jennifer. I love her thick, black, wavy hair which is loosely tied back. In contrast to our paleness, her complexion is rich ebony.

Her job was as a radiologist at the Mayo Clinic in Minnesota; this information made the eyebrows of myself and Mike shoot up, and we both let out an, "Impressive!"

So, just among us three, we have an oncologist, surgeon and radiologist. We've clearly been selected for our skills. But this is no time for false modesty, we all seem to be good looking. And a glance around the room makes the penny drop. As quietly as I could, I remarked on this to my new colleagues who agreed.

It feels more like a prison than a refuge down here. The strong military presence, of what we have now ascertained is the Global Force Allegiance (GFA), is oppressive. Yes, if arguments or dissent grew in such a confined space, which is likely, it would be catastrophic. But even considering this, it's heavy-handed. The GFA was supposed to be a peaceful alliance. Clearly, that was completely ineffective. And now they've branched out into the aggressive kind of peace-keeping, ruling at gunpoint.

Jennifer grabbed my hand, squeezing hard as she drew a deep breath. "Just how long are we going to be here for?"

We all paled as the answer formed; surely for a considerable length of time.

I felt sick but forced down the lunch they gave us. It was a broth, so wasn't too hard to do. I will need to keep my energy up.

When I got back here to my room I curled up on my bed and let the tears fall - only when alone was it safe to do so. I may never see my family again. Pain ripped through me like a sword and a thousand stab wounds puncturing my soul. I muffled my wail with my pillow, hoping nobody would hear.

I don't know how much time has passed but I finally stopped and began to write before I forgot anything.

One question burns through my brain in bold, red lettering…why us?"

Rongo looked around the room. Her students were hugging each other or holding hands, some were crying.

"We know her truth. And we will not forget or neglect the honour of her sacrifice," Rongo said, her voice cracking.

"We will honour her," the ones who could audibly formulate words agreed.

They made their way back to their parents. Aroha shut herself in her room, crying alone like Dr. Rachel. But her mum came in after just a few minutes. Without words, they clung onto one another, both in tears.

"Mum, she knew. Right from the start she knew," Aroha said when she could find her voice.

"And she carried on. Fortitude, my darling."

"Fortitude."

Aroha requested some time alone, which her mother respected. She spent that time contemplating the deeper meaning of fortitude; *courage in pain or adversity.* So often had she chanted the tribe's motto. But never before had the words struck her so deeply.

She could only hope that if ever faced with such devastation, that she would show the same resilient attitude. Aroha feared the opposite would be true, but then she'd never been so cruelly tested. Nobody should undergo what those people did.

A bunch of people got evacuated; the greatest of their kind, leaders in their field. They were taken to safety. And they founded what became their tribe. That did not even begin to cover what had happened but was the gist of what Aroha had heard thus far.

Adults didn't talk much of the hardships. They hinted at hunger and hard work, giving them sanitised lessons. This? She owed the founders so much more than she could ever conceive of giving.

With the weight of responsibility weighing heavily on her shoulders, Aroha attended the next reading with greater reverence.

Rongo, having checked with the class, began the reading.

"17th March 2069

I have missed a day here. Apologies, but it was impossible for me to summon the will to write yesterday.

They announced the meteor has hit at last. The wait is over.

Whether their version or mine is true, a great disaster has now befallen our planet.

We are to understand the severe impact this has had already and will continue to have in the upcoming days. Confinement to our hidey-hole is set to continue. And still, contact with the outside world is not permitted.

Should nuclear war have broken out, I find myself hoping my family were in the strike zone. I feel sick at writing those words. But the alternative is so much worse. The famine which has already seen rations reduced would surely intensify. A lingering, slow, painful death is so much worse. But I am wishing death on my own flesh and blood. And I cannot escape the feeling that makes me the worst person alive. I do not deserve to be here.

I do not say this lightly. All day yesterday was spent crying. Mike must've heard my animalistic wailing from his room. He had to argue his way into my room. The guards didn't want to let him through, but he pleaded humanity. He refused to allow someone in so much pain to suffer alone. I think he may have punched someone; there were lesions on his knuckles.

Mike was so patient. He sat quietly, physically holding my pieces together with a reassuring arm. I must've fallen asleep at one point as I woke up, my head on his chest. But then guilt flooded me. Here I was, lying in the arms of another man already. I know he meant well but Mike has made me feel as if I have betrayed Theo already, and I would never do that. How I wish he was here with me, along with Joshua and Ella. My babies! Why won't they tell me about them? I need to know. Don't they understand? I don't want to live without them. I can't. I won't.

20th March 2069

Mike forced me to eat breakfast this morning. It's been days since I ate, so my health has weakened and yet I'm unable to care. Again, he fought his way into my room. I am useless here. My skills aren't needed. They should've let me die with my family. Why couldn't they?

My mind is muddled; I can't decide which is more selfish. To wish my own demise, or to carry on in my family's name even though they're not with me and may be dead. Mike tried to tell me they may yet be alive and we will be reunited and I'd be sorry not to live to see that happen. He's right. But I don't dare to hope. Not wanting to give in, just on the outside chance he's right, I've forced some food into me. Heaven knows I don't want to, but I will carry on, for them. For now.

22nd March 2069

We've still not been allowed outside. Has there been a global tsunami courtesy of the meteor? Or have the guns fallen silent? Why can we not go out? Surely all threat is passed now.

Over dinner last night, our little trio whispered about nuclear fallout. We are all of the understanding that the lethal fallout lasts 24hrs.

If the war broke out on the 17th, it'd all be over by the 19th at the latest. I suspect sooner. So, by today we should be permitted to go outside. And that's being overly cautious.

There's never been any mention of nuclear armament in the southern hemisphere. Fallout shouldn't even be a problem here.

Who was involved? America was first and worst hit by the bee extermination and famine, but nobody escaped. Europe, Asia, The Middle East, Africa, Australia, Oceania – everyone suffered. And most have nukes. We could be among the last humans alive.

I wonder if the people in the other evacuation centres survived. Where are they; nearby or a different country entirely?

And how many people are still out there, on the surface? If there are any local refugees, will they need my help? Has anyone been damaged by radiation this far south? Maybe that's my purpose here.

Jennifer has managed to speak to some of the emergency medics. Our scrubs are not the same here, by the way. There are only red ones for the emergency teams – those who people need to seek out first. And us, the clinical teams in green.

But nobody seems to have been called upon. No influx of injured has been rushed in. Useless seems to be the consensus.

Let us out. Let us go and do our jobs where people actually need us, please."

"Why were they not allowed out, Rongo?" Aroha asked.

"That's a good question. Why do we think?"

Lots of scrunched noses and pondering, "hmms," went around the room.

"Was there nuclear fallout?" someone suggested.

"We don't think so."

"Umm…was it because people were scared?"

"That's one possibility. The people inside were scared but the people outside would have been too. We think the battles happening down here intensified as people panicked even more about depleting food stocks."

"It must've been scary," Aroha wondered out loud.

"And dangerous. The GFA forces were trying to preserve the human race. The people inside might've been killed if they'd gone out, don't you think?"

"Was it so bad here?"

"It looks like it, sadly. You were taught about nuclear winter a little bit in history. Do you remember what happens?"

"It gets cold," Gerald offered.

"Mm-hm, big clouds of dust blocked out the sun. Temperatures dropped. Even fewer crops grew. So, even although we don't seem to have been hit by missiles, we did starve, indirectly affected by the global nuclear strikes."

General moans of disgust were emitted along with winces.

"Starvation," a few murmured.

"It's a horrible way to go, for sure. I think we could all do with a positive reminder. Let us feel the comfort of community. We all love each other and are safe here. Come on, hug it out."

Each student linked up with their neighbour in a group hug.

"Alright, we still have a lot to get through, so let's move on," Rongo announced once the students were calm.

"28th March 2069

Another week has gone by and still we're down here, living like moles. The medical crews have demanded learning sessions. We have been permitted supervised sessions so that those who need to can brush up on first aid, basic and emergency procedures. We need to do something. The aim is to start moving about more. There are more levels to this compound, and we're going to volunteer to go through the different sections, performing medical check-ups.

At least with so many nationalities, nobody teases me about my northern accent. I worked in London once, and the ridicule was savage.

We can all speak English, so that's what we converse in. I suppose I should be grateful the Powers That Be didn't decide to use this as an exercise in ethnic cleansing. It's of small comfort when our liberty has been taken from us.

Jennifer and I are making use of the gym here, as we've been encouraged to. Keeping active is a vital distraction. Being alone for too long is not fun. Every thought turns to my family, and I go in circles, wondering if they're alive or not, grief and guilt alternating within my conscience. If left to fester, it's crippling.

The not knowing is the most torturous, but try as I might, the people in charge here refuse to tell anyone any details. Not even when we can expect to be allowed out. I must suppose that all answers would be negative.

Mike only had his parents, not that that's any less dreadful, really. Jennifer had close friends, her mum, aunties, uncles, cousins. She even spares a thought for her ex-boyfriend.

I had in-laws, but no blood relatives outside my own children. Did any of my former colleagues get sent to a bunker?

We are all in suspended grief, fearing the worst, hoping for the best. There isn't a single person in here who has not been separated from someone they love. United in grief, brought together by disaster.

3rd April 2069

Another week. I am trying to spare pages now. With no sign of us being set free, it's probably wise to try to save my diary for important details. We must be set to be down here for the long-term.

A few medics were taken to the farming level to carry out the proposed health checks. Hydroponics plants are being grown, which is why we're still getting vegetables and salads, I think. And this has firmed up our suspicions of a long-term plan.

To be fair, we're getting better nourishment here than home. Forgive me for not celebrating that too wildly.

They get to wear jeans there. I'd say they're lucky, but that's not the right word down here.

The Diary Directive is now more an information-gathering mission than ever.

10th April 2069

I'm not sure how much longer my watch battery will last. It's been my only means of seeing the date. I've started a tally chart/calendar on the back page of this book.

We get a late breakfast and dinner, so can mark the days off from that if nothing else. Obviously, no daylight shines in. It's not like we have windows.

There must be generators as we have artificial light. Our room lights go off when we should sleep and on when we are to wake up.

Mike rolled his eyes at me when I showed him this diary. Apparently, you may want to know what it looks like down here. I suppose describing it makes it real, hence my avoidance. But for posterity's sake, here's the details...

You can't really see any evidence of the caves; only a few exposed walls show their grey, rough surface. Mostly, it's long white corridors, dimly lit, supposedly conserving electricity.

Mike thinks fresh air comes down via ventilation shafts. I'll take his word for it.

My own room consists of a bed, a small cupboard for my uniforms and a tiny table. Floors, walls, ceiling, linen – everything's white.

Cleaning crew come and replace the bedding and scrubs regularly. Our meagre underwear supplies are our own responsibility. A basic laundry room has been supplied for that purpose. Nobody wants to swap undies, even clean ones, so there's no complaints.

We have communal toilets with individual cubicles which provide little privacy. I never liked using public toilets before, and this is just what they're like.

There are separate female and male showers, which we're allowed to use once per week. We have a toothbrush, toothpaste, towel and flannel. Oh, and a hairbrush. No deodorant. We're trying to get used to the natural odour. I miss my bath and body spray.

The lack of makeup seems to be more of an issue for others. I don't mind that so much. Who am I trying to attract? Nobody. And my hair is accustomed to being tied up in a ponytail anyway.

If I think about it too much, I start getting claustrophobic. Suffice it to say, it's not terribly different from a hospital. Lots of white corridors.

In all fairness, I've not seen too much.

The hydroponics area was apparently well lit; I suppose it has to be for the plants.

I will try to explore more either myself or via the reports of others as we do our rounds."

"It doesn't sound very nice," Gerald commented as Rongo reached the end of the diary entry.

"I don't think I'd like it, would you?" Rongo extended the question to the group.

"No," they chorused.

"Eww, and no deodorant," Hana whined. "Was what they used in the Before the same as ours?"

Rongo responded, "I think it was different from our wax and oil mixes, but it probably wasn't too dissimilar."

"What's makeup?" Aroha asked.

"People used to paint their eyelids and lips in colours. There are books with ladies with red lips and brown or blue on their eyes in the library."

"Why?"

"I suppose they thought it looked nice. There doesn't seem to be any other purpose."

"Weren't their markings enough?"

"Not everyone had markings, Aroha. In fact, the only ones with ones like ours were the Maori from what I can find."

"Huh. But at least ours aren't just decoration, they mean something. Painting over your face for no reason is weird."

"Compassion, Aroha. We do not judge others. Their ways were different, but that does not make them wrong."

"Sorry, Rongo. It's just strange. I didn't mean to sound negative. I'm only trying to understand."

"There is certainly a lot to think about. What do you think they'd make of us? That can be your meditation focus this evening."

On their way back down the hill, Aroha stared across her homeland. Domed structures called biomes housed important plants which needed protection. The Peace rose had taken on its own superstition, and was the best looked after plant of all, for fear peace would fail them without it.

All the bungalows were on the surface. Daylight was in abundance, even if it was through protective glass.

Outlying fields housed their crops and livestock. Barns gave refuge and storage where needed. The animals couldn't stay out too long but always went inside when appropriate, seemingly by instinct. Sometimes the farmers needed to offer them encouragement. Large sails would be pulled over some fields daily too.

Large metal containers collected rainwater and run-off from the mountain for all their needs. And there were some buildings for the hydroponics plants. A lot still struggled to grow in the soil, even now.

Out of sight, the biomass processing plant was working hard, turning waste into energy.

Fields of solar panels could be seen in the distance. And the arms of windmills spun, glinting in the evening sun.

Who would want to live any other way?

Chapter 4

The next morning, before reading class, being relieved of chores for this period of study, Aroha went to the library. Some of her classmates had had the same idea.

These prised tomes had been rescued from a town by the first settlers. Carefully, Aroha took down some books from the shelves and carried them over to the tables and sat with her friends.

"Look, here's a painted lady," Hana pointed out, pushing the book across the table.

They laughed. "Look at her bright red lips."

"Look at what she's wearing," Hana added.

"Be kind," Aroha admonished.

"I don't mean to be nasty. It's just funny though, isn't it? Her dress goes out so far around her."

"It does seem to use more material than is necessary. But then in the Before, I don't think they minded about waste."

"Mum says they had showers every day."

"Dr. Rachel said about showers in the diary yesterday. She seemed shocked at only one a week. But a flannel wash is just as good and uses so much less water. Why would you have a shower every day?"

"Waste."

Aroha sighed. "They couldn't have known better. Someone should have shown them."

"Look, here's a hospital," one of the boys announced, pointing.

They each took turns to inspect the image.

"I suppose that's not so bad," Aroha said with a shrug.

"Those cities though, so many people. It looks so busy," another student put in.

Aroha took the offered book and turned the pages. "Look at these. They were called flats. People living on top of one another in tall buildings."

"That's so weird. How could they?"

"I don't think I'll ever understand. It was just so different."

"I think it's nicer here."

"I'm not going to argue with that. Mum says that it would have been very noisy."

"And probably smelly."

"I reckon."

They continued looking in books and sharing information until it was time to get changed for their reading session.

Once they'd performed the rituals, Hana's hand shot straight up.

"Yes, what do you want to ask?" Rongo invited.

"Dr. Rachel said the bees had gone extinct. But that's a lie."

"That's a very good observation. But Dr. Rachel had promised honesty. I don't think she knew. It certainly seems true that *most* of the bees had died, certainly in the northern hemisphere. That's why all their crops failed. And people starved even in the Before. We know it led to wars. And those wars got worse and worse until they launched nuclear weapons, which led to the devastation."

"But we have bees."

"Yes, there were some here which survived. And our village was supplied with hives by the builders. There must've been some surviving colonies in New Zealand, or perhaps they were kept safe in secrecy especially for us. Either way, we have been very lucky. They help pollinate our crops, herbs and flowers and supply us with honey for food and medicine."

"But why did all those people have to kill each other?" Aroha asked.

"Fear and anger were the ultimate weapons, Aroha. Imagine being that hungry. And then your neighbour has food but won't share."

"Why not?"

"Because then they wouldn't have enough."

"I don't think I understand, Rongo. I would always share."

"And I pray we never do truly understand. May we never know such calamity. Alright, are we ready for today's reading?"

The obedient heads nodded, so Rongo turned to the diary.

"17th April 2069

We are still trapped here. It has been over a month. There must be other reasons for our continued confinement. I fear for the survivors. Perhaps there are still skirmishes?

We have the means of growing food and still have dried stores. Does anybody else? Or is the human species withering like the crops in the fields?

How long can we exist like this? I am frantic to get out, to see the sun. There is still no news of our loved ones. Part of me cannot resign myself to their demise, yet my hope is in shreds. My arms ache to hold my children. My lips long for Theo's. If only I had known that last goodbye was my final one, I would have held on tighter and longer, told them how very much I loved them. Instead, I whisper to them in the dark, my soul reaching across the miles, maybe realms.

One of us on this floor, Kyoko, is a microbiologist. She has no access to her advanced testing equipment but managed to argue her way into the kitchens to check hygiene was being observed. Our health being of prime importance, she gained entry.

Vast kitchens of steam greeted her. They are definitely cooking for a greater number than just those we've seen in the canteen. Are there more canteens on other levels? Do we eat in shifts? Why do we never meet?

One of the wood-fired ovens was broken and an engineer was working on it. Smoke went up a chimney, so the ventilation shaft theory for incoming air seems sound. We're getting water somehow. Surely, tanks would have run out by now. There must be a filtration system.

So, we have kitchen staff, medics, farmers and engineers. GFA soldiers are here, obviously. Are there firemen? I suppose military police suffice for law enforcement, not that the law has been clearly defined. No killing or fighting, go where you're led without question; that about covers it.

There are no shops, no money. We are given what we need, treated like barn hens. I still have no true purpose. I'm bored and useless.

19th April 2069

Tomorrow would be Ella's fifth birthday. Has she made it? Will she be able to celebrate? Is she crying that her mummy isn't there? I am. The cakes of my childhood parties have long been absent. But we would still have had presents and tried to get a little extra food to celebrate. And I'm not there.

Sorry, I must stick to facts of what is. The Diary Directive is not for my personal pain. It is to record the truth. My loss is my truth, though. I cannot escape it. But I will try to record only the findings of our new existence.

Cleaners obviously come into our rooms whilst we are at breakfast, as our few effects are neatly placed, and new sheets/clothes are left out. The personnel are always gone before we return though. It is odd how we're still so segregated; ominous and oppressive.

We have managed to discover a few dentists among our medical faction.

A few medics have been called upon for slips, trips and falls. Only a couple of more serious injuries have required specific medical attention. Most of the time we're still idle. This cannot continue indefinitely. There's only so much time a person can spend in the gym or walking in our allocated space.

If radiation is a factor in 'the outside', there could be an increased risk of cancer, so I could well be called upon in the future. I'm going to ask if there are any labs so I can further my research, or at least review any cases if any such records exist here. I have to suppose there are, given the aim seems to be to protect our little unit of humans. They can't expect us to conjure these things out of thin air.

21st April 2069

*There was resistance to my proposal, which was
expected. Data is on a need-to-know basis. Do these
guys know we're not all military personnel?
Anyway, I managed to persuade them I could sit and
review existing cases without contravening any
directives. My deepening depression must be evident
as when I pointed out I need something to do, they
seemed to appreciate that. An idea has been buzzing
around, and so I ventured to request specific types of
cases, just in case there's a choice.*

*Today, I was taken to a more brightly lit room. It was
tiny. A small table and chair were the only items of
furniture. On the table were two lever-arch folders,
an A4 notepad and two pens. Isn't it ironic that I, of
all people, now complain of an overly clinical
environment? There is NOTHING personal here. No
homely touches. It really is a military prison.*

*In the folders were computer printouts. Perhaps they
have computers somewhere, but not for the likes of
me. On the spines of the folders were reference
numbers, like the Dewey Decimal System found in
libraries. My heart skipped a beat, hoping beyond
hope that somewhere here is a vast library of vital
human discoveries catalogued and preserved.*

Proteogenomics research has made massive leaps, and our cancer cases had been reducing as a result. Understanding the root causes of cell mutation was essential. And there were case notes in the first folder, demonstrating different approaches. Nothing new catches my eye; I knew the basics already. But if nothing else, it fills my empty hours, and my mind is occupied. For the first time in months, I am immersed in work.

The second folder contained naturopathic oncology case notes. It's fascinating. Treatments to flush out the lymph system seem sound. But boosting the immune system with vitamins, botanics and diet – obvious in its simplicity.

By combining the proteogenomics idea – the molecular level, and the naturopathic theory of the body's environment, you get a holistic approach, treating the whole person. Change the gut health and the environment, so the proteins don't have what they need to grow in the first place. But perhaps we can take that even further.

Furiously scribbling notes, the day disappears. Eventually, my armed guard come back in to escort me out, forcing me to abandon my notes. They told me they will be filed, but nothing was to leave the room.

I don't suppose it matters, as much as I hated leaving them there. The future is yet to be written. We have no idea if any of this is relevant. It occurs to me, that with increased risk of radiation, perhaps we were even selected according to DNA, not only for general health but without the susceptible genes to cancer, perhaps other diseases too.

If I had been consulted, I confess, this would have been a suggestion. Not that it would have been a palatable one. But when given a limited choice of which humans to save? Well, the gloves have to come off. Or should that be the surgical gloves go on? A little medical humour to lighten the dark thoughts.

Perhaps I was wrong before. It may not be ethnic cleansing per se but it is, at best, genetic manipulation."

"And so we see Dr. Rachel trying her best to help mankind, even in such a confined space," Rongo added.

"Her future was so uncertain. It must have been so scary for her. She was literally kept in the dark," Aroha commented.

"That's certainly true. She was working blind, without knowledge of what equipment or which diseases may occur. As an expert oncologist, her whole life had revolved around helping others. And all that was taken away in a heartbeat. Isolated, underground, knowledge kept from her…it must have been soul-destroying. We can see she's bored and frustrated. Do you pick up other emotions from her?"

"Sadness," someone suggested.

"More than that, despair," someone else added.

"Yes. She mentioned in that last entry about depression."

"Why did her leaders not organise talking sessions?" Hana queried.

"They didn't have them."

"What?"

"There are books on counselling in the library. That was like our talking sessions. But that was only for people who were already depressed, and it was just between two people."

"Just two? But how does that help? When they had so many more people to live with, why did they not have more in these counsellings?"

"It seems odd to us, doesn't it? Every week we have our community meeting and we are all encouraged to speak in the talking session. We then all help support when and where required. But they did not have that in the Before. Historians have researched the information we have, and it looks like the individual had come ever more into focus."

"But no one person stands alone," Aroha stated.

"No, not here. But there? There, in the Before, they did."

"That's maybe the saddest part yet."

Chapter 5

Alone in her room before dinner, Aroha tried to imagine being alone like Dr. Rachel had been. It didn't make any sense. She had her husband and children in the Before. And they lived in a big city. Despite her best efforts, she just could not see how people could be lonely individuals when so surrounded by others.

"I love you," she told her mum, walking out of her room and into her arms.

"I love you too. How was it today?"

"It doesn't get easier, does it?"

"No. But each day, do you not feel more thankful for what we have?"

"I do, I really do," she replied, squeezing harder.

"Come on, time for grub."

Her dad joined them as they made their way to the dining hall.

Looking around, Aroha looked at her community. There were no uniforms, just whichever clothes were best for their daily task and/or what was comfortable. All were one.

Each villager took turns in cleaning and farming duties, thanks to a rota system. Each had a specialism, ensuring all skills were passed down and continued. Some had an aptitude for making clothing or parts, whilst some were better at fixing human or animal bodies and so went into medical or veterinary practice. All were important, all had a vital role to play.

Their elected leaders were honour-bound to listen to the community. Their job was to keep the peace at the community meetings if they got a bit lively and to introduce new measures where appropriate. They were no better or worse than anyone else.

There were no military forces standing by with guns. Nobody forcing them to go anywhere.

Testing her newly-realised freedom, Aroha took a walk after the evening meal.

"Do you need a friend?" Gerald asked, catching up to her, his grin wide in his hollow, freckled, latte cheeks.

"Honestly? I don't really know."

He took her hand as they walked side-by-side. "It's a lot to take in, huh?"

"Sure is. I reckon I just need some fresh air."

"To remember you're not trapped under the earth?"

"Something like that."

"Come on, let's tour the fields. We can check the cows as we go," he suggested, leading her in that direction.

The sun was low in the sky. They grabbed hats and overcoats from the pegs at the door for warmth.

Cattle lowing carried across on the wind as they approached the fields. Some cows stopped munching to look up at their visitors.

"To think there wasn't even any grass in the immediate After," Gerald wondered out loud.

"There was no anything, I suppose."

"Figure we'll hear more about that too."

Aroha sighed. "There's so much we didn't know. I don't think I want to either."

"Don't be that way."

"I mean it, Gerald. It's horrific."

"Exactly. We need to know this stuff if we're to avoid their mistakes."

"I don't think I'd ever treat anyone that way."

"Best to be sure though, eh?"

Tilting her head, she acknowledged, "I guess."

Gerald lived in a bungalow close to her, and they'd naturally grown up as friends, attending school together. But soon they would have to decide which path their futures would take.

Squeezing Gerald's hand, Aroha led him beyond the animal fields, towards the cliffs. Patting the ground next to her as she sat, Aroha settled into a cross-legged position. Her friend joined in silence.

Waves crashed against rocks below them, hissing and rumbling in their dance. Tuning into their song, the pair closed their eyes and took deep breaths. The sweet, salty tang tickled their nostrils and filled their lungs.

"Dear Source," Aroha began, "thank you for the clean air that we breathe and the freedoms we have."

"Thank you for the food in our bellies and the smiles on our faces. Blessed be our families and community," Gerald added.

"Our thanks unto you," they chorused, their palms on the ground.

Not needing to say anything, they sat, quietly observing the power of nature about them. After a while, Aroha's head flolloped onto Gerald's shoulder; her wild, black hair trailing down. Shifting position, his left arm wrapped around her back, their heads connecting.

"Beauty is all around us," she said with a deep, satisfied sigh.

Gerald moved so he could look at her properly. "It truly is," he whispered.

Their gazes locked and breaths were held within their chests.

Aroha bit her lip, unsure what to say. This was Gerald, her friend. Cheeky, fun, Gerald, the joker. But now the twinkle in his eyes did not speak of mischief. It spoke to her soul of a deeper longing, one which made her glow from the inside.

She saw him in a whole new light as if the setting sun were a torch highlighting something hitherto unseen.

Coughing, Gerald looked away. "It's getting late. We'd best be getting back."

Aroha nodded, words failing her. She felt rejected, without really being able to explain why. Had she wanted to kiss him? Maybe if he'd not looked away she would have. It was a shock, wanting to kiss her friend. Did he want to kiss her too? Why did he not? Maybe it was just her, and now she'd made him uncomfortable.

Unsure what to do, she ruffled the short crop of hair on the top of his head as if nothing had changed.

"Come on slowcoach," she called, starting off at a run.

There was nothing else for it, Gerald gave chase. They were both laughing, trying to draw breath by the time they reached home.

"Um, well, er, I'll see you tomorrow?" Aroha said, swiping her hair behind her ear.

"Um, sure, of course."

There was an awkward pause before Gerald turned around and sloped off to his own bungalow.

A frown furrowed Aroha's brow as she pushed her door open.

"There you are. Are you alright?" her mum asked.

"Hm, sure," she mumbled, walking past.

But Aroha's mum stopped her, placing a hand on her shoulder. "Not so fast, young lady."

Rolling her eyes, Aroha turned back to face her mum.

"Do you want to talk about it?"

"About what?"

"Aroha, if you want to pretend everything's fine you might want to tell your face."

"I'm not really sure what it is myself."

"Was it your lesson?"

"Only at first. I went for a walk on the cliffs, y'know, to…"

"To feel free?"

"Yeah, that. Just to breathe."

"And Gerald? He needed to do the same?"

"If you saw, why are you asking me?"

"I only saw you two walking away together after dinner."

"So? We're just friends."

"Aroha, I don't like your tone. What happened?"

Aroha looked to the ceiling and groaned. "Argh, we just went to meditate. But then, I don't know. I kind of wanted to kiss him. But he looked away and then we came back here. Alright?"

"And now you feel confused?"

The girl's hands washed over her face. "Mum, this is really embarrassing. I wanted to kiss him, my friend. And he didn't feel the same. Nothing happened."

"So, you feel hurt?"

"Stupid, I feel stupid."

Her mum's hands wrapped around her, and a kiss was planted on the top of Aroha's head. "Don't. You have nothing to feel stupid about."

"How could I feel that way? I mean, it's Gerald."

"You're growing up. And that comes with grown-up feelings. Gerald is someone you know and trust. It makes perfect sense."

"Except he doesn't feel the same way."

"Oh, I don't know. I wouldn't be so quick to judge. Did it occur to you he may just be as surprised and shy as you?"

Aroha stretched back, narrowing her eyes as she looked up at her mum. "You reckon?"

"Could be."

With fidgeting fingers rubbing her arms, Aroha made her way across to the reading house the next morning. She had avoided even looking at Gerald at breakfast but was now walking close to him with no idea what to say.

He was looking at the ground as he walked. Aroha wondered if he would ever forgive her. She'd clearly messed everything up, jeopardised their friendship. There were no cheeky winks or grins promising playfulness today.

Aroha's hand flew to her hat as the wind tried to knock it from her head. The gusts were strong, and they all walked a little quicker to their destination.

All eyes turned towards Rongo as she began the reading.

"28ᵗʰ April 2069

I have been allowed to continue my research which is a relief as it focuses my mind away from the negative.

Still no news on the outside. Still no trips to the surface. Still no idea of how much longer we are here for.

A brawl broke out amongst the maintenance engineers the other day. I only know this as some of our colleagues were called to patch them up. Fortunately, there were no serious injuries. It seems the GFA intervened.

Things are starting to fracture; this is surely a sign of that. Worry and boredom are mixing into frustration and anger. I feel it within myself and see it in my friends and across the dining hall. The armed forces are twitchy. I don't trust those trigger fingers.

I cannot bury myself in research. It is a good distraction, but it solves nothing. There are matters which should not be ignored. Is it for me to intervene? Why not?

We are being bullied, imprisoned and isolated. One fact keeps coming back to me…

WE ARE SUPPOSED TO BE THE FUTURE OF HUMANITY

And what sort of world are we building here?

Our liberty has been taken. We are ruled by unseen dictators. Who died and made them king/queen/president? They are as unelected as they are invisible. Who are they to decide how we live?

We have an opportunity here. A real learning point. If we are ever to change our future we must learn from our past.

But what can be done?

There are so many unknown factors.

Who, what, why, where, when? The age-old questions are largely unanswered.

29th April 2069

As if in answer to my thoughts, today, we had one of those demeaning conferences. The speakers were rolled out. They don't fool me; I am under no delusion that these people have any real power, they are mere puppets. However, they are what we have. For now.

They informed us that the outside has been more severely impacted than predicted. It is not safe to go out.

Well, I suppose starvation and a nuclear winter would lead to civil unrest amongst those still clinging onto life!

We are not to worry, apparently. This scenario was covered in Emergency Planning. Oh, the committees and talks they must have held, deciding our fate without consulting us.

They are opening more of the bunker, or what they call the underground city. One could argue this could already have been done. Like all things, it was judged on a 'needs must' basis. We were taken down to view this glorious place.

Consider me well and truly gobsmacked. A large, green space. There was a large light tunnel and numerous smaller ones coming down, channelling what must be actual daylight onto real trees and ferns. UV lights supply the rest of the needed rays.

Breathing deeply, the air felt fresher, sweeter. Without worrying what anyone would think, I walked to the nearest tree and hugged it. Something I never thought I'd do. But I was just so damn grateful to that beautiful tree for existing. Others did the same, which helped me feel less weird about my own behaviour.

We were permitted an hour of free time to enjoy this precious gift. There's even an area of artificial turf there, large enough to play a little kick-about. Not quite a football pitch, but enough to have a small game. And a basketball court stands to the side. We're being encouraged to make use of this space. It's almost as good as being outside.

The hydroponics folk must be helping keep this greenery alive too. It's amazing how anything can live down here at all, but this is a whole other level.

3rd May 2069

A few days later, and we've started using Green Space more. Some footballs and basketballs have been supplied, and we're all enjoying some fun. At least, before the guilt kicks in.

Once we're alone, we each seem to reflect more. My next-door friends, Mike and Jennifer have both mentioned this too. And the remorse we feel is suffocating.

Survivors are surely having a terrible time out there. And here we are, eating sufficiently if not extravagantly, and having fun. Without witnessing conditions in the outside, we still appreciate that the contrast must be stark.

The other medics echo our sentiments. We all long to go to the surface, see if there's anyone there who needs our help. Can we really not bring anyone else into our bunker? Our pleas to this fall on deaf ears. Our rations and living spaces have all been carefully calculated.

But selfishness is not in our nature. We weren't given the option, nobody asked us. I suppose none of us would have come if they had. We would always have put others first. And yet medical attention will be required; that's a certainty. Still, we're extremely uncomfortable with this whole situation. We have pledged to preserve life, taken an oath to do so, in fact. Leaving people to die is not right.

My anger is bubbling. I must remain calm. Think happy thoughts.

Now that games are starting to be played, we're trying to suggest tournaments. Of course, that will help us see who else is down here. But we're calling it friendly competition to the GFA. Exercising off some excess energy and aggression. They're considering our proposal!"

"She's so clever," Aroha admired out loud.

"Dr. Rachel certainly felt compelled to help. Her sense of injustice is growing, can you sense that?" Rongo quizzed the class.

"Oh yes," Hana agreed, "She's angry, isn't she?"

"Anger is there. What else?"

"Frustration."

"Guilt."

"Pain," Gerald added.

"Yes, good. Pain. She's hurting. And threatened. She doesn't like all those guns. When you mix up all those negative emotions, we're likely to strike out."

"Like an injured animal. One of the farm cats had hurt her leg, she was limping. I bent down to look and see if I could help, but she hissed and then scratched me," Aroha shared.

"Yes, just like that. When we feel vulnerable, we might lash out, protecting ourselves from getting a more serious injury," Rongo explained.

"Did these GFA people not know that?"

"You'd think they should. Maybe they were distracted? Maybe they weren't listening to the people?"

"They can't listen if they're not there. Dr. Rachel doesn't know who their leaders are. It's so strange. How can they rule that way?" Aroha asked.

"They have eyes and ears in their soldiers."

"Then they should have spoken more to them."

"I'm sort of glad they didn't," Rongo said with a smirk.

The group chuckled.

Once class was over and they reached the atrium, Aroha tugged on Gerald's hand.

"Can we talk?" she whispered.

Looking around before he responded, Gerald agreed, "Alright, but I haven't got long."

Aroha's brow furrowed. What could he possibly have to rush away to? He'd not looked at her all day. Fine, she'd avoided him at first, but it was getting silly now.

Going to an area where they could talk alone, Aroha forced her courage to the surface.

"Look, I'm sorry about yesterday, OK?" she spurted.

"You are?" he asked, looking up from the floor.

"I don't know what came over me."

"Yeah, it was kind of weird, huh? But nothing happened."

"No. Quite. I just wanted to make sure you knew it wouldn't."

"Well, that's a relief. I wouldn't want to jeopardise our friendship," he explained.

"Exactly."

"And the timing's all wrong. There's just so much to think about right now."

"Glad we're on the same page. It's just too complicated."

"Right."

"Right," she echoed.

"Good."

"So we're OK then? Friends?"

"Friends."

A quick hug later and they went their separate ways. But an awkward feeling remained in Aroha's gut. They had talked it through, yet for once, it hadn't seemed to help. Had she been honest with him? With herself?

Clutching her stomach, Aroha realised that perhaps she did truly want more and Gerald didn't. She'd given him the opportunity to say if he did. He had declared against anything other than friendship. A tear trickled down her cheek.

Chapter 6

"12th May 2069

Two months we've been in here now. And today is a Sunday. The chapel has seen increasing usage, but today was really busy. We all seem to be turning to a higher power for answers.

No one religion dominates. We are all free to practice whichever faith we believe in. An interfaith minister presides over Sunday service, holding a quiet space for us to issue our own prayers to our selected deity.

No pipe organ accompanies hymns. No chanting echoes from spires. Even our religion seems different down here.

I rarely attended church before. But that was then. Now, I offer thanks for my survival and prayers for my family and my friends' loved ones, for all still out there.

We're told great clouds have blocked out the sun, that the temperatures have fallen. True, a large enough meteor could cause that, but the suspicion of nuclear war grows. But why lie? Are the people in charge here culpable? Are they ashamed of their actions? Have they saved themselves before more worthy members of Earth?

There may be very clever people down here, capable of performing essential duties. But are we the best? Where are the kind people, those who have performed excellent acts of philanthropical goodness? Are they here?

One good thing about a growing congregation is that people from all parts of this subterranean city take part.

There are all sorts. Arts and crafts people who can spin wool, make and mend all manner of useful things from bowls to clothes. Not being rude, they seem quite hippie-like. That's not a bad thing. Just not necessarily what I expected.

Miners have been preserved. Butchers, teachers, chemists are among us too. It seems that every useful profession has been thought about. Talk about building a civilization!

But you know who's absent? I've not met or heard of any lawyers yet. Clearly, they don't serve any purpose. Or perhaps the leaders were worried they'd have the tables turned on them?

As our network of...ponderers has grown, we've been able to discover more. And it is abundantly obvious now that we have the building blocks of an entire city. There can be no doubt that they always planned to have a fully functional society in reserve. Vomit rises up my oesophagus!

At least the Green Space allows for a little more communication between us. Rumours are spreading wider. Dissent rises!"

Community Day arrived in Fort Itude, so classes were paused. The whole village helped out with the essential tasks first thing, so the rest of the day could be spent in rest and/or celebration. A little extra food was provided at midday meal where the chatter was a little louder than normal.

The weekly Talking Session followed the meal, where anyone with general concerns could be heard. The comparison was not lost on Aroha. She mulled over the way the leaders in the diary had acted. Why had they not done this? Stupid. They must've been stupid.

Trying to smooth out her worry lines, Aroha started to make her way to the exit. Chastising herself for still holding negative judgements on the leaders in the bunker, she wanted to walk it off.

Without thinking, her feet led her past the animal fields again. Realising where she was heading, she turned up between two fields, avoiding treading over ground she'd shared with Gerald. One of the horses whickered as she approached its paddock.

"Sorry, I don't have any treats today," she apologised to her four-legged friend, spreading her arms out wide.

Dipping and raising its head, the horse snorted, giving his neck a shake. Aroha stroked the brown nose pushed towards her.

"At least you're not complicated," she told him, "Bit of food and you're happy."

Aroha physically jumped back and yelped as a voice answered her.

"I dunno, nothing in life needs to be more complicated than that."

Charles laughed as he saw her reaction. "Ah, gee, I'm sorry. Didn't mean to scare you. I thought you knew I was there."

"Clearly not," she answered, straightening her hat. "You were hidden by horses."

"I was just checking hooves. They all seem good. Reckon I'm about done here. Where you headed?"

"I don't know really."

"Do you want company or you deliberately on your own?"

Aroha sighed. "Maybe you could join me? My own thoughts don't seem to be clearing on their own."

Pocketing the hoof pick, Charles bounded over and launched himself over the fence. Aroha couldn't help but admire his athleticism. There was a roundness to his jaw which softened his otherwise chiselled features. A kindness always shone from his hazel eyes, a slight green shimmering through the brown.

All the girls were wildly attracted to him, Aroha included. But she knew he wasn't interested in her. He'd been with Lizzie for a while now. No, he was just being nice by offering to walk with her. It was what people did; see someone alone, offer to be a friend. There was no good reason for her stomach to turn somersaults.

"You're going through the Diary Lessons, aren't you?"

"Yep."

He scratched the back of his head, his fingers reaching through his long, wavy, black hair. "Phhw, tough."

"Yep." Why could she not say any more than that?

"That why you out here on your own?"

"Yep."

"I remember when I started learning our history. It's a lot to take in. I mean, it's not like I didn't know before. But there's so much more."

"Sure is. It's making me evaluate my own life, I guess." There, a complete sentence.

"I know what you mean. Where you at?"

"Dr. Rachel has been inside for two months, and they've just got Green Space."

"Well, I won't say anything. No spoilers."

She nudged him as they walked. "Oh, go on. Just a hint."

"No, no. The leaders would string me up," he told her, laughing.

"Tease."

Clearing his throat, he asked, "So, what's really on your mind?"

Biting her lip, Aroha looked away. "Everything."

"Gee, that's a lot." He chuckled.

Wiping her hand across her forehead, Aroha explained, "I don't know. It's just appreciating more exactly what sacrifices were made. How many were left behind? So many died."

Charles stopped. Taking her hands, he looked directly into Aroha's dark eyes. "That's not our fault. We would never ask for others to go through that. You need to remember that."

"I know, I do. But I can't help feeling guilty." A tear trickled down her cheek.

Charles wrapped his arms around her, and Aroha felt his sturdy chest beneath her cheek. For the first time all week, she felt safe and secure. A deep sigh escaped her as she revelled in the hold. This only prompted his hand to be rubbed up and down her shoulder.

Forcing herself away from the luxurious comfort, she looked up at him with a weak smile. "Thank you."

"You're so generous, Aroha. So sweet to think of others all the time."

Her mouth gaped. He'd noticed?

"But sometimes you need to think about you." His rough fingers stroked her cheek.

"I think that's part of the problem. I've got to choose my path soon."

"That's not such a hard choice is it?" His eyes were still focused on her, melting her insides.

"Um, no, yes. I don't know. It was easy for you."

"Animals and me have always got along," he said, shrugging. "Just like you and people."

"I thought I knew, before. But hearing about Dr. Rachel, I'm not sure I can ever live up to that."

Again, that featherlight touch was on her. How could someone so strong be so gentle? His hand was on her shoulder. "You don't have to be her. You just have to be you. And I happen to think you're a pretty good person, Aroha." His voice trailed into a hoarse whisper at the end.

"You do?" she asked, gulping.

"Uh-huh."

His face inched closer to hers. This couldn't be happening. His lips parted. Hers mirrored his. She took a deep breath in. She could smell his own scent mixed with the horses he'd spent the day with. His warmth heated her.

"No," she shrieked, backing away.

"What? What's wrong?"

"I can't." Her eyes widened.

"Why?" he asked, stepping closer again.

"It's wrong."

First Gerald, now Charles? What was happening?

"It's natural," he said.

"Natural? What about Lizzie?"

"What about Lizzie?"

Hot stinging shot through her hand as she slapped that gorgeous cheek. "How could you?"

"What? Aroha, I don't understand."

Shocked and embarrassed, Aroha ran away crying, heedless of his calls after her.

Charles caught up with her at the meeting house.

"I'm busy, Charles," she said as firmly as her quivering voice would allow.

"Aroha, please listen to me."

"I don't see why I should."

"Argh, you're so stubborn sometimes."

"And even less so now," she said, turning to walk off.

His hand grabbed her elbow. "You don't understand."

"You OK, Aroha?" Gerald asked at her side.

"Fine, thanks," she answered, taking the opportunity to walk away from them both and towards her family.

The boys were glaring at one another in a stand-off. One of the elders led them both out the room. They both looked sheepish as they shuffled back in several minutes later.

Pretending not to notice, Aroha continued to speak with her girl friends.

As if she didn't have enough to worry about, the boys had to start being weird.

Aroha trudged to the Reading Room the next morning, her mind trying to sort through the confusion of her own life. Her concerns over what happened in the Before mixed with her own worries until she wasn't sure which way was up.

The serenity of the meditation before the reading was a welcome one. Pushing all conscious thoughts away, Aroha focused on her breath. Nothing existed, everything existed. Life ebbed and flowed. And she just was. Aaaahhh!

After the usual question and answer session, during which, Aroha remained silent, Rongo began the reading.

"20th May 2069

Today should be Joshua's 7th birthday. But like Ella, he won't be celebrating. I've spent the day curled into a ball in my room, trying to hide my misery from the others. The pain rips through my soul. The anger lashes out at an enemy I cannot see; how dare they take his life? He is gone, isn't he?

I know it wasn't just my own family. So many lives just gone. And lied about. Innocent children! Please, just tell us the truth, you owe us that much.

12th June 2069

Another month has passed. I am sorry, but I find myself unable to write many entries. Life has settled into a dull routine. And there's no point fighting against the machine. The cogs keep turning.

The guards never let anyone else into my room again. Supposedly, it's to deter any close interpersonal relations. No sex! Well, I suppose we don't want more mouths to feed now, do we?

I've made a point of greeting the guards. I'm not sure whether it's more that I'm trying to be subversive and/or irritating, or whether I truly need to find something human within them. They stand on duty as rigid as any palace guard. The most I get back is a tight-lipped, "hmm" with a head nod. Except for one.

The chap who's most often outside my room is starting to soften. I got a, "Good morning," last week.

It got me thinking, as tough as it must be for us, perhaps it's worse for them. I never see them relaxing or talking. They're clearly career soldiers, but I'm sure even they must be feeling the pressure. This situation isn't natural for anyone.

I've been allowed to continue my analysis of case studies. And our network is growing. None of us 'civilians' seem thrilled with being here. We're drip-fed tiny bits of information. And still, we don't know how much longer we face in this hole.

My writing is devolving into moaning again, so I'll stop. See; this is why I don't do more. I've become a whinge bag. And I don't know what to do.

19ᵗʰ June 2069

Over the past week, I've gradually got a name out of my guard; Fetu. Pronounced FEH-too. He says it so nicely. Short for something like Fetuilelagi, which I can't quite grasp. He even flashed me a quick smile when he told me; a row of bright white teeth shone against the contrast of his tan skin. The severity of his usual scowl was suddenly swept away. The man was revealed from behind his usual menace. He's really quite attractive when he's not glowering.

At last; a sign of something other than automaton in these GFA guards. I will continue my greetings and see what I can make of it. Slow and steady. I don't want him to clam up again."

Chapter 7

Having talked to her mum, Aroha came to a decision; to do nothing. At least about the boys. Now was not the time to think romantically. She'd make it clear to both of them that they were just friends. Her head wasn't in the right place to explore further at the moment.

These things are easier said than done, however.

But lessons continued.

"25th June 2069

Fetu smiled before I even had the chance to wish him good morning today. His head bobbed in a sort of salute/greeting. Funny how such a small action can feel like such a massive victory.

I replied with a cheery, "Alright, mate," and continued on my way to Green Space.

He responded with a, "Good morning," but at my retreating back.

Having not expected him to speak, I'd not stopped.

OK, so, I may have glanced over my shoulder and noticed him looking at me. Let's not get too ahead of ourselves. I don't think he's ready to reveal any great military secrets or have a cosy heart-to-heart. It's just nice to see humanity is all.

Anyway, I continued to my destination and had a pleasant stroll, breathing in the fresher air, chatting to some friendly folk.

A sense of calm seemed to envelop me for the briefest moment.

29th June 2069

OMG, I hardly know what to write or how – my hands are still shaking.

We were at dinner, as usual, when this lad stands up. Judging by his accent, he was American.

"Who are you?" he shouted.

There was stunned silence at first. But then someone else stood and repeated the question.

What happened next was more like a footie match of old – chants of, "Who are ya?" along with stomping feet and the banging of trays. Feeling left out, I confess to rising up too.

It all happened so quickly. A rush of people joining together, demanding knowledge of our captors. At least, I presume that was who the question was aimed at.

Just as swiftly, the GFA forces took action. Three of them leapt on the instigator, pinning him to the ground. He struggled, kicked and swore. Others came to his aid, trying to tear the soldiers away. They were dealt sharp blows with elbows and feet. More GFA swarmed in and herded us out, but it took time.

The initial guy was still standing his ground. Fear made him fiercer, and he was calling them out. Defiantly, he demanded to be taken to our leaders so he could tell them what he thought to their face.

The soldiers tried to cuff him, but he struggled every bit of the way, lashing out, spitting, anything he could.

He was given a warning. Repeatedly, they told him to comply. I heard and saw it all as I shuffled along, trying to reach the doors.

One shot rang out. It echoed around the dining hall. Just one. That's all it took.

Screams erupted from every mouth and the crowd surged towards the doors. The American lay dead on the floor, blood trickling out. And we were squashed in panic, scrambling to get free.

It was difficult to keep my balance. Several times, I was almost pushed over. It was a struggle to breathe as my body was pressed tightly between others.

Even outside the dining hall, chaos met me. People were fleeing along corridors and I didn't know where to run to. The decision was taken from me as I got swept along with the throng. Running to keep up with the others, I fled but stumbled. Down I went with a thud. Feet pounded the floor around me. God, I thought I was going to be trampled to death. A foot crushed my hand as the person rushed in terror, one of many.

Curling up in a ball, I cried, awaiting my death, unable to get up. Feet and legs were all around me. Stomping and screaming filled my ears.

I could see my room; so close yet so far. Within spitting distance of safety, that is where I would die and join my family. That one thought brought consolation amidst confusion.

More shots were fired, orders were barked. And I remained, being kicked as people ran from gunfire.

Hands gripped my shoulders, pulling me to my feet and guided me down the corridor, then we went through a hidden side door. My ears were ringing in the sudden silence, my body screaming with lesions and contusions.

But new fear crept in as I stood in complete darkness, trying to catch my breath. A scream got trapped in my throat.

"Shh, keep quiet, we're safe here," was whispered to me.

Sure, right. No problem here. Why the hell would I not trust this disembodied voice?

A hand found mine and pulled me further into the darkness, along what must be a tunnel. I had no option but to follow, my feet stumbling, unable to keep up even at a walking pace. Everything hurt. Rough rock scraped my hand as I tried to feel my way.

We turned a corner, and another door opened – I heard the click of the latch. I gasped as it closed behind me.

But then a low-light torch was finally switched on. I gasped again. The illuminated face looked like something from a horror story, lit up from underneath. Only parts of it were revealed. High cheekbones appeared hollower in shadow. Eyes glared down at me.

"Are you OK? Are you hurt?" he asked.

Slowly, my mind pieced together the bits of face with that voice. I'd only heard a few words from those lips before.

"Rachel? It's me Fetu. Are you harmed?"

I hadn't answered him. Was I alright?

"I think I'm in shock," I muttered.

"We'll rest here for a minute until our way is clear."

He put an arm around my shoulders, maybe just to keep me on my feet.

I could only hear his side, but he had conversations on his radio. He must have an earpiece.

In a whisper, I asked him who he was protecting when he stopped the radio chatter. He told me to keep quiet. But being me, I didn't. I tried to ask him who was in charge, where his duty truly lies, if we're the future, aren't we the ones who need protecting? Stony silence was all I got for my trouble.

*I pointed out that with so few humans left, shooting **any** of them is probably a bad idea. Blindly following orders is no longer sensible. If he doesn't even know who's issuing those orders, the same rules surely can't apply.*

Still nothing came from his lips.

Who's soldier is he? Does he even know? If there's no government now, which there probably isn't. then who are the GFA answerable to? Who's pulling the strings? He could be the puppet of a madman.

I asked if he's aware that the majority of us are civilians. Innocents. We're not the enemy. We shouldn't be kept like prisoners.

It was only when I told him that they weren't fooling anyone, that we know a global nuclear war had clearly broken out and not some random meteor, that he got irritated.

He shushed me, repeating it was for our own safety, that we mustn't be found there. There was something in his tone which brooked no further argument. I shut up.

Besides, he started talking into his radio again.

Once he was sure the corridor was clear, he led me out, but not to my room. We wandered down more dark corridors and came out near the medical centre. He left me there, waiting to be seen.

Once I was finally checked over, iodine applied, stitches put above my eye, my hand taped up, I was allowed to return to my room. The long walk of shame – GFA soldiers were everywhere. Eyes followed my every step. It was a relief to finally get 'home' and close my door.

There were many casualties, the nurse treating me had confirmed, recognising me. She wouldn't allow me to assist. Part of me knows she was right to deny my help, but I still felt like I was neglecting my duty.

Tragically, there were five people dead by the end of the day, including The American. The others died in the panic. I'm lucky not to be amongst that statistic. And it could have been worse. I'm choosing to believe those numbers and that nobody else was shot. One death by shooting is bad enough.

wtf happened here?

30th June 2069

Will I ever be able to describe the terror I felt, being ushered into the hall for a meeting today? I physically shook as we were herded together. Just yesterday, I was almost trampled to death, my injuries still stand as testament, fellow inmates were wounded, some killed. And now we were put in the same vulnerable situation?

I hadn't even gone to breakfast; too scared to face the dining hall.

They read us the riot act! That phrase has never been more appropriate. Any form of protest is absolutely prohibited. We have seen what the outcome is. Death! Yes, they actually told us we will be shot if we attempt to repeat such action.

So much for saving us!? It seems that only the meek shall be rewarded with life in the bunker. Fuckers!

What the hell is this place? Hell being the operative word.

4th July 2069

My injuries are healing in accordance with expectation.

The atmosphere is very strange today.

The Americans among us would usually be celebrating American Independence Day now. But we're not even sure if there's a country left at all to celebrate. And even if there is, fireworks were such a big part of that celebration, what do we do?

Understandably, it's caused a lot of upset and frustration. Even more than normal.

The rest of us have joined in sympathy. It's made us realise we may no longer be nationals of anywhere. No treaties protect us. What is out there? Is this it? Is this now our home? Are we now one tribe of Bunkerites?

This hell hole is no home. I won't end my days here. I'll find a way out or die in the process of trying.

4th July continued...

I spoke with Fetu on the way back to my room. I went too far.

I pushed him for answers he warned me I wouldn't want to hear.

But the tension was driving me crazy, I had to know. And he knew; it was in his eyes.

~ Is there anything left of the UK? ~ Is my family safe? Two simple questions.

He hesitated. But pity swept over his face before he could disguise it. A howl echoed through the corridor before my world went black.

My eyes opened to a pair of dark brown ones looking at me under a furrowed brow. A hand was gently stroking my sweat-dampened hair. He told me everything was OK. He was wrong.

My country was obliterated. Liverpool had a direct hit. My life is over.

I doubled up in pain, tears coming out with my screams. The noise alerted my neighbours, who both came in with no guard outside to stop them. Fetu kept apologising; to them or me, I'm not sure. Just sorry over and over again.

My babies. My beautiful babies. My heart was torn out and smashed on the ground, trodden on and destroyed. All this time I'd been strong, hoping against hope. Even when I knew deep down what must've happened.

"Tell them," I demanded of Fetu. "Tell them what you told me." I was yelling, fire glaring through my red eyes.

He realised his error. The terror in his face was there. A soldier, afraid.

But it was too late. He'd gone against his orders and there was no taking it back. How I wish he could. I was wrong. Not knowing was better than this.

Mike sunk to the floor, not in a faint, but a sudden need to sit. His hands washed over his face. No London. His family also wiped out.

Fetu wasn't so sure about Minnesota, but he told us that there was very little left of anywhere in the northern hemisphere. He made us promise not to tell anyone else. He doesn't know what will happen to him if anyone discovers he's said anything.

We agreed his life may be in danger; with a plentiful supply of soldiers, they'd have no qualms killing him. Now we're faced with a massive moral dilemma.

He went back out the door, praying his absence hadn't been noticed. But if questioned, I merely fainted. Oxygen is lower here; fainting isn't uncommon. Decreased diet, oppressive heat, increased exercise as we try to fill our days with activity – all this leads to an almost certainty of people passing out.

The three of us need to decide what to do whilst grieving the loss of family and country. I try not to swear in this diary, but this really calls for a full 'what the fuck?'

What are we supposed to do now?"

The teenagers were hugging each other and crying. Aroha was glad Gerald had sat next to her now; his arms were holding her as much as hers were holding him.

Rongo handed out handkerchiefs, wiping her own eyes with one as she went.

"Geez, Rongo, why do we need to hear this?" someone asked.

89

"I know it's hard. Stick with it. It's so important. Through Dr. Rachel's diary, we know what really happened. The dreadful, brutal reality. What we have to be thankful for. And what we need to be mindful of."

"It's too much," someone else sobbed.

"I'm so sorry. These lessons aren't treated lightly. We know they're not nice. But you won't forget them either. We never should."

Giving her students time to gather themselves, she continued.

"5th July 2069

Jennifer, Mike and I are distraught. Thank goodness we have each other. We were allowed to stay together overnight. Fetu only separated us once his shift was coming to an end.

We've decided that we don't want to inflict this pain on anyone else. Especially if it means putting someone's life in danger. The burden is heavy upon us. But I'm already dragged to the floor with grief anyway.

We won't lie either. We'll allow and maybe even encourage speculation. Let people come to their own conclusions in their own time. People will naturally reach a point when they will suppose their loved ones are dead, if they haven't already.

Knowing for certain hasn't helped any of us.

I don't know if I can carry on.

"19th July 2069

Fetu allows our little group to convene in one of our rooms each time he's on shift. He's indebted to us, for sure. But maybe it's also compassion.

He seems genuinely sorry for our distress, covertly shares it. Maybe that's why he spoke out? He must've lost people too. Maybe he needed someone to share his grief with. I don't think the soldiers would be allowed to discuss such things. He seems so alone.

Fraternising with civilians is definitely not permitted, and he dare not risk joining us, but I think he wants to. We'd welcome him.

Mike is the most pragmatic of us. He says we have to continue in order to honour the dead. To make their lives meaningful. They should not have died in vain. It is up to us to make a better world now.

That's an even heavier burden than the one we were already carrying. But it echoes my own feelings.

If we truly are the future of mankind, we need to do better.

21st July 2069

Today's religious service was my first opportunity to speak to a group. Once the minister had led us in our individual prayers, I made my way to the front, my knees wobbling. I could have been signing my own death warrant.

Unsure what I was going to say, I started speaking. "Everyone, I'd like to take a moment. I'm thankful for this space to offer up prayers. But I want to expand on that, if you will let me. We've been here for over four months now."

The GFA forces gripped their guns and warned, "No protests."

I splayed out my fingers, holding my arms up. "I don't mean to start a disturbance. I just wanted to ask you how you're feeling."

Well, that caused a whole rush of talk. For a moment, I thought they were actually going to shoot me.

I begged people to speak one at a time. The guards shouted for order. Eventually, my inmates complied.

As expected, people spoke of their frustrations and concerns. My hope is that the soldiers will report back to whoever's in charge.

They have a problem here and they need to deal with it. If we can't speak to them directly, this seemed the best way to give feedback.

One of two things will happen; we'll start getting more information or all groups will be disbanded and privileges revoked. Either way, something will happen. Either way, there will be repercussions."

"Bloody hell, that's how Talking Sessions started?" Gerald wondered out loud.

"Mm-hm, that's how they began," Rongo replied.

"Geez."

"Quite something, huh?"

"I'll say."

"Such a simple question. How are you feeling? Can you imagine the courage it took to ask something so mundane?"

"She must've been terrified," Aroha said. "She could have been shot. There were soldiers with guns for crying out loud. They'd already killed one person."

"No wonder her knees were wobbling," someone else commented.

"I don't think I'd have been able to stand, let alone walk up there and talk like that," another added.

"She had nothing left to lose," Aroha noted.

"Exactly," Rongo agreed, "Dr. Rachel at that point maybe didn't care so much if she got killed. She knew her family were dead, her home destroyed. And she didn't know if that meant being stuck in the bunker forever. And her sense of justice wouldn't allow her to remain silent. Why not try to make a difference?"

Murmurs of admiration and bemusement travelled around the room.

"OK, I think that's a good place to stop for the day. Let's head back," Rongo announced.

Aroha reached for Gerald's hand and gave a squeeze as they walked along the path together. "Thanks for being there today."

He squeezed back, casting his gaze towards her. "Always. You're my friend."

His few words warmed Aroha's heart, filled her with peace and comfort. Always. She felt the truth of his words. No matter what, they'd always be friends.

A mixture of trepidation and excitement buzzed through Aroha's veins the next morning, Dr. Rachel was bound to do something awesome now. She couldn't wait to find out what.

"24th July 2069

Well, they have responded.

We were called into a section meeting today. We were admonished for our flagrant bolshiness. The speaker's eyes were targeted at me as he spoke. My cards are now clearly marked, a trouble-maker in their midst. Good. So be it.

On this occasion, they have decided to answer our enquiry whilst strongly discouraging any further similar action. We are, at the same time, to believe they have our best interests at heart. They do not want to cause upset or panic. Every care is being taken to ensure our needs are being met at this difficult time.

We stand on the edge of annihilation. The meteor (yes, they are sticking to that story) caused chaos. Earthquakes, tsunamis, volcanoes, the works. Wow; impressive work there, rock! Some nuclear plants subsequently went into meltdown. Ahh, that would be how radiation got into the atmosphere, eh? Not the thousands of nuclear missiles. God, they think we're stupid.

Anyway, because of all this, as they've already told us, a large dust cloud is in the atmosphere, plunging us into winter. They kept reminding us we already knew this. They're not hiding anything. Honest!?

They've been doing some calculations. The destruction is on an unprecedented scale, which is why they weren't sure before. They wanted to check their predictions were realistic before sharing. Course they did!

They reckon we'll be stuck in here (not their exact words) for around five years.

Jeers of incredulous, "Five years?" bounced off the ceiling and walls.

*We've not been here five **months** and it's too long. YEARS?*

They urged calm. But when in the history of humans, has saying, "Please remain calm," ever actually had the desired effect?

If our seats weren't screwed to the floor, I think some of them would have been hurled. Rage burst from every person. Shouts, screams, foot-stamping; it all got out of hand. One soldier shot across our heads. What the actual…? They actually shot at us again. Above us, fine. But in our vicinity. And didn't that just shut us up? Damn them, it worked. Fucking bullies!

The speakers are just as unhappy as we are. They never intended for us to be here that long. But comprehensive contingency planning means we have what we need to survive. Whoop-de-doo. Surviving is not the same as living, people.

I could have kissed the person who asked who's pulling the strings. Thank you, whoever you were for not making me ask. I'm already in their bad books.

The response was clearly evasive. Given our violent reaction, it is best they remain anonymous for now. We were assured that an expert committee regularly convenes. It's not just one person, and they are doing their best to keep us safe.

"What about the survivors outside?" someone else asked. I love that person too.

The expected answer of only having enough provisions for the people already here was rolled out again. I could have written their script.

When another asked if we could go out at all, of course, they got a big fat no. Unless we're fans of toxic gas clouds, being mobbed and freezing cold temperatures, it's best avoided. Sarcastic arseholes!

So, that's it, there's no way to help those poor bastards outside. It makes me sick to my stomach. People must literally be dying of starvation and God knows what out there. What are we doing? Sitting nice and comfortably in here, not raising a finger to help.

"We can't save everybody," they said. We could at least fucking try! How can anyone sit by when they know such suffering is taking place? I just want to punch them!

I have no words. Nothing describes this loathing. This hatred. It cries out to my inner lioness and she is roaring."

Never before had Aroha felt such hatred. It was scary how she could feel so strongly about people she never had and never would meet. She walked back in silence, negative energy seething out of her. Not even Gerald dared to get close.

As soon as they got back, Aroha changed and headed out for a run.

"Rack off," she told a stunned Gerald who was about to knock at her door.

Where was this anger coming from? She puffed out her breath as she ran towards the cliffs. Not helping others went against every natural instinct she had and all she'd been taught. It was plain wrong. But why so angry?

There was nothing she could do about it. It wasn't her trapped in that bunker. Ah, there it was. Trapped. Her parents were expecting her to make a life choice, but it wouldn't necessarily be the one they wanted. Was she really free to decide? Was she not trapped in her own way?

All her life she'd been given the same lessons as everyone else. But now she was to go into her specialism. Her family were all in medicine before her, and they expected that's what she'd do. Aroha had too. But now?

She wasn't a great hero like Dr. Rachel. And having heard the stories of what her mum had done in emergencies; could she too be that calm under pressure? Her emotions were all over the place. She was striking out, getting angry. These were not good reactions in a medic.

Maybe she could become a teacher? No, she needed something where she could use her hands. Maybe a seamstress? No, she wanted to help more. Making clothes is useful, but not direct enough. Every thought seemed to throw up a wall in her mind, and they were all closing in.

Was she choosing a course because it was expected of her?

Her footfalls continued their relentless pounding on the ground as she turned back towards the fields.

A cry chilled her veins but had her feet speeding up in the direction it came from.

Seeing blood dripping out of Charles' hand, she sprinted over. "What happened?"

"I was fixing this fence, but I…got distracted. The saw cut through me instead of the post," he said through clenched teeth, hissing between words.

Aroha whisked off her jogging jacket and wrapped it around the boy's bleeding hand.

"Press down on here for me. We're going to walk over to the stables. It's not that bad, but we need to clean your hand, OK?"

"Sure."

They walked briskly across the fields, Charles wincing as they went.

"Right, where's your first aid kit?" she asked once they got to the building.

"Over there, behind the door," he answered, pointing with his head.

Dragging a stool across to the low tap, Aroha sat Charles down and shoved his hand under the running water, making him hiss again.

Getting a sterile cotton pad, she stopped the water and held it to the wound and lifted his arm up. "Keep this up for me a sec, OK?"

He nodded.

"How do you feel? Any dizziness?"

"No. I'm OK. Just feeling like an idiot."

Checking for any clamminess, she held her hand to his forehead.

"My arm aches, can I bring it down yet?" he grumbled after several minutes.

"Not until I say."

Walking in, one of the senior grooms exclaimed, "Shoot, I thought I heard something. You OK?"

"Yeah, Dr. Aroha here has it all under control."

"So I see. Need any help, young lady?"

"I think we're good. Just waiting for the bleeding to stop properly."

"I'll let you get on with it then," he said with a wink before busying himself with jobs around the stables.

After fifteen minutes, Aroha inspected Charles' hand before applying some tea tree oil, smoothing honey over and finally wrapping a bandage around.

"There. That should hold you," she told him.

"You're amazing," he said, looking up at her.

"Oh no, don't you get all kissy again. I still don't think it's a good idea."

His face scrunched up. "I wasn't going to."

"Sure."

"Look, since you brought it up, I wanted to tell you Lizzie broke it off with me."

Aroha tilted her head to the side. "She did? Well, I'm sorry to hear it."

"She just wanted to use me for her first. As soon as I gave her what—"

Aroha held her hand up. "Way too much information."

"Sorry. I didn't want you thinking I was trying to snag you both at once, y'know, before."

"Fine. Not that it matters. Still don't think I'm ready for this discussion though. We're just friends, end of."

Charles rolled his eyes. "OK."

"I think you'll live. I'm going to leave Fred here to make sure you get home safely," she said loudly over her shoulder.

"Don't you worry. I'll see to him," the groom called.

"Thanks, Aroha. You really did an amazing thing here," Charles told her, holding up his hand.

"Glad I could be of help."

Turning to walk away, Aroha couldn't stop the massive grin spreading across her face. She was going to become a medic. Not because that's what she owed to all those people who lived before. Not because her family pushed her that way. No, Aroha felt it in her blood. It's who she was – a healer.

Chapter 8

"*27th July 2069*

Fetu snuck into my room last night. He wanted to caution me to moderate my behaviour. I assured him that I'm not stupid, but nor will I be cowed. If people are suffering, I will speak up for them. His concern is very sweet though.

Whilst he was here, I quizzed him on the bunker's layout. He's only been to a limited amount of places though. The GFA don't even trust their own soldiers apparently. But he did tell me there's far too many guards, doors, levels and barriers to even attempt reaching the surface, and I would be killed if I so much as tried. It's so frustrating, but some things have to be accepted. Even getting around this zone is hard enough. As much as my heart struggles against it, I have to face facts; I cannot smuggle in or out.

So, my concentration will have to focus on the people here. I couldn't leave so many behind anyway. And where would I go?

There is something very wrong with our societal structure. But there is also such a thing as biting the hand that feeds you.

There must be something we can do. I'll have to speak with my friends to come up with a plan.

28th July 2069

Today was a prayer day. The guys and gals with guns gripped them firmly as I once more walked to the front, slowly with my hands spread out. I explained my aim was not to cause trouble, my actions came from a place of benevolence. The guns remained held at the ready.

I called for us to rearrange ourselves so we were sitting in a circle.

"This is a safe place," I announced, looking pointedly at the guards, daring their intervention.

We spent our time simply talking, mainly about how we feel about the prospect of being here for five years. Ideas were tentatively offered how we can maybe improve our life. If we're here for such a long time, then we wanted to have a better sense of community.

Amongst ourselves, we have formalised this weekly gathering. That following our time for religious worship, we will hold a talking session where we're free to discuss our concerns, whether our leaders are listening or not. It is our right to free speech, which we all agree should be upheld.

29th July 2069

Well, that went down like a lead balloon.

We were gathered in our sections and firmly reminded that no form of public protest is allowed. The proposed sessions following weekly worship would be viewed as such.

"It is not free speech, it is a clear and deliberate attempt to undermine authority. Furthermore, any further discussions on the matter will be considered an act of sedition which will not go unpunished."

"But we just want to talk. To be heard," Mike piped up.

"Rest assured, we listen. But we will not be dictated to."

"Nor will we," someone else shouted. There was a scuffle in that direction and a man was dragged screaming from the room.

"This is a survival situation. We cannot emphasise enough the precariousness of our way of life. A system has been put in place to ensure your safety and survival. It will not be threatened. To do so is to jeopardise the future of humanity."

The divide between them and us is growing. Tension is mounting on both sides.

Fetu came to my room again this afternoon.

"Please, you have to stop this," he urged, holding my hands.

I appreciate his apprehension, but my resolve remains, and I told him as much.

He tried to tell me there are means and ways of doing things. That he's on my side. He doesn't like what's being played out here, but we must be careful.

This is important though.

30th July 2069

Even my friends have urged me to see sense. We must remain low key. No more public demands for assembly.

I tried to protest that I just want to talk. But they pointed out the authorities view talk as dangerous. One of Jennifer's contacts saw the medic who was dragged from the room yesterday; he was covered in bruises.

Not wanting anyone hurt in my name, perhaps, for now, we do need to be seen to comply. Argh!

4th August 2069

There is clearly a hunger for interaction. The congregation today was larger than ever, perhaps as a form of passive protest to the authoritarianism at work. A reaction to brutality.

Nobody moved to convene after prayer. I did not move a muscle. There were even more soldiers present and I felt their eyes boring into me throughout the service. Outwardly, I was all meekness, head bowed, lips firmly closed, just one of the sheeple under the steeple.

A ball has been set in motion. It's rolling on its own.

9th August 2069

A woman approached me in Green Space today. She spoke in hushed tones of the long-forgotten footie tournament. I agreed it was a good idea, but we'd need to quietly arrange it ourselves. My name wasn't to be mentioned, although I'd help where I could.

Perhaps on Tuesday, the medics may turn up at the 5-aside pitch. She's from the farming zone, so maybe there could be a team from there who happen to turn up after lunch. It must appear to be circumstantial. An accidental occurrence.

13th August

Another uneventful yet large congregation were at prayer this Sunday just gone.

And what do you know? Two teams happened to play a little game of football today. I wasn't there myself, but I'm told the farmers won against the medics. I'm not even sad about that. Secretly, I'm punching the air, jumping for joy, head over heels happy they played. I'm so proud of us.

21st August 2069

The chapel is going to need an extension at this rate. It was overflowing this week.

After breakfast this morning, five farmers happened to meet five cleaners in Green Space. How did that happen?? The farmers, so I hear, remain the victors. But conversations are happening on and off the pitch.

It occurs to me that we're missing a pub. How nice would it be to have a swift pint after the match? Not that I can remember the last time we had that at home, let alone here. But that would encourage…discussion. Heaven forbid!

There are little inter-sectional games happening in between, so the tournament is less conspicuous. The exercise is beneficial if nothing else.

Me? I'm mainly continuing my research, noticeably on my own. Nothing to see here, guv. lol, Mike and his London speak is rubbing off on me.

Talking of whom, I'm sure he and Jennifer are exchanging flirty glances. Maybe it's wishful thinking."

"Aww, how lovely. Mike and Jennifer together," Hana cooed.

"Yeah, when they gonna get busy?" Gerald asked.

Rongo raised an eyebrow at him. "Eager for some action, are we, Gerald?"

The poor boy just blushed.

Aroha considered love forming in that environment. Everything was in place to discourage relations of an intimate nature. Yet here were two people, attracted to one another despite that. Love really is the strongest force in the universe.

At breakfast the next morning, Aroha sat next to Gerald.

"Are we OK?" she checked.

"Course."

"I'm sorry about the other day."

"It's forgotten."

"I just need to know. Do you like me?"

He rolled his eyes. "I thought we'd done this. We're friends, aren't we?"

"No, like me, like me?" she asked, biting her lip.

Gerald looked down at his food.

"I'm not asking you to do anything about it. The timing's all wrong, for a start. I just need to know, should the time come that you feel the same way," she blurted out in a rush.

Honesty, she was going for honesty. No shying away from the topic.

Still not looking up at her, his head hanging low, he mumbled, "Yeah, I like you."

Before she could say anything else, Charles came bounding over.

"Hey, have you seen what our medic did? She saved my life," he announced, waving his bandaged hand at Gerald who actually looked up, silently working his mouth.

"What? She didn't tell you?"

"I've not had the chance yet, and it's not like I saved your life, drama queen."

"Saved my hand then."

"Not even."

She turned her face back to Gerald, Aroha teased, "I was out jogging and heard a girly scream."

"A manly yell," Charles corrected.

Ignoring him, Aroha continued, "So I went racing over. He'd just sliced into his hand a bit. Nothing major."

"There was a lot of blood for nothing major," Charles defended.

"Really, it wasn't that deep. It's not like you cut an artery, Charles. Get over yourself. All I did was clean up the wound and dress it."

"Yeah, but you did a great job. Man, you should've seen her. So calm. She knew exactly what to do. It was amazing."

Aroha blushed. "It was just basic first aid."

"Lucky you were there," Gerald said at last.

"Right place right time, I guess," she said with a shrug.

"Charles, will you stop waving that thing around like an injured hero and come and eat breakfast?" his dad called.

"I was just thanking my own hero, actually."

"Eh? What's this?" her mum asked from further down the table.

Blushing more, Aroha tried to dismiss the subject. "It was nothing. Can we just eat?"

"Come here, Charles. Let me take a look at that."

Her mum carefully unbandaged the boy's hand and inspected the injury before wrapping it back up and sending him back to his parents.

"That was a very neat job, Aroha. Walk me through what you did."

She spoke of her actions, as requested, but with reluctance. Her mum was beaming at her by the time she'd reached the end of her tale.

"I'm so proud of you."

"Muuuum," she whined, wriggling in her seat.

"Don't be so modest. It couldn't have been easy seeing your friend bleeding out like that. But from what I heard, you kept your cool and dealt with the situation in…hand."

Aroha rolled her eyes. "That's so corny!"

"Couldn't resist," her mum replied with a wink. "But I mean it. You need to give yourself more credit."

"Well, it did make me realise something."

"What's that?"

Gerald tensed next to her, taking a sharp intake of breath.

"I'm going to be a medic."

Gerald exhaled. Her mum got up and came running around the table to give her a hug.

"Geez, mum," she moaned whilst hugging back.

Taking the opportunity whilst Aroha's mum was walking back to her seat and her dad's attention was diverted, Gerald kissed Aroha's cheek.

"I'm proud of you too," he whispered.

Smiling broadly, her eyes shining, she whispered back, "Thank you."

General chatter took over as they ate, the community enjoying one another's company.

Aroha started to walk in the direction of the library after breakfast, but Gerald caught up to her.

"You got a minute?" he asked.

When she nodded, he led them to one of the quiet break-out rooms.

"You can't just ask me stuff like that and not say anything."

"Sorry. Charles kind of interrupted, then my mum…"

"I know that. Look, I just wanted to see where you are."

She looked all around the room, anywhere but at him.

He took her hands in his. "I'm over here, Aroha."

"Sorry. I just…"

"Look, here's how I see it. You like me, I like you, right?"

She nodded.

"And I don't think much is going to change that. I've…my feelings…they've just been getting stronger."

Aroha's gaze locked on his. "They have?"

"Yes. And don't pretend you haven't experienced the same. I do notice some things, you know."

"So why didn't you kiss me the other night?"

He scratched the back of his head and sighed. "I chickened out, OK? You were right there and it was suddenly all real, everything I'd been hoping for, and it was kind of sudden."

"I thought maybe you didn't like me like that."

Gerald sighed out a nervous laugh. "How could you think that?"

"I don't know. We've never said or done anything about it. I thought maybe it was one-sided."

"It's not. But I respect if you don't want to do anything about it right now. Just know I'm here for you, even if it is just as a friend."

Her arms wrapped around his shoulders. "Thank you."

He held on tightly, holding her close.

Walking side-by-side but not holding hands, they went to the library together to study their past before thinking about their future.

In class, Aroha sat a little closer to Gerald than she was accustomed to, their knees touching. Just that hint of contact seemed to reassure her of his presence, but also sent tingles through her body.

With considerable effort, she focussed on Rongo as the reading began.

"26th August 2069

Yesterday's congregation maintained its numbers.

I had thought perhaps the show of faith, pardon the pun, was a one-off. But I'm happy to report that everyone seems determined to stand up against tyranny.

It may be small steps. There's a limited amount of leeway. The leaders are probably wise not to show themselves. But I wish they would. We only have the speakers' word that there even is a committee. For all we know, it's one lone mad billionaire in charge, some Howard Hughes character. Or it may be a misguided Mother Theresa type. The point is, we don't know.

Not knowing who your life is in the hands of is terrifying. Especially if it is an eccentric rich person. They may change their minds and cut off our air supply and decide to do away with his failed experiment at any given moment.

And without the knowledge of who, we have no way of judging our safe boundaries. Just how far can we push it? Exactly what repercussions would there be if we go too far?

Misgivings aside, the farmers retained their title today against the cooks in the latest football match. They're really good. I saw them in action today. It occurred to me one of them may even have been a professional player. How would we know? Just because we've been shoved into designated roles, it doesn't mean we didn't have different lives before. Anyone could be anyone.

1st September 2069

The amount of sad faces at worship each week is growing. Gradually, we all seem to be accepting our families, friends, loved ones are probably all dead or dying. It's excruciating. I can't be the one to confirm their worst fears, to bring that much misery down on them. Besides, I don't know for sure. I can't speak for everyone.

But the congregation is losing hope either way. The whispered prayers are increasingly for whichever God to look after souls, not lives; to welcome them into heaven.

My own prayers are kept within, merely thought up to a God I'm not even sure I believe in. Surely, He would have stopped this happening? How could an almighty being stand idly by and watch his creation destroy itself like that?

4th September 2069

I got talking to one of the skilled crafters today as we stood watching the farmers win yet another match. They're unstoppable!

Said crafter is a metal worker and self-declared hippie, named Paul. His kind green eyes, gentle smile and encouraging manner had me discussing more than I intended. Our conversation circled back to the God question.

Paul believes everything happens for a reason, and that this is all part of some greater plan. That the human race needed something drastic to occur to instigate change.

I pointed out nothing had really changed socially. Most of the population has been seemingly wiped off the face of the planet, and we're still answering to a form of government, only this one's unelected so it's worse.

He agreed that, on the face of it, that is the case. But maybe there are fierce lions sleeping in our pride. That we just need to bide our time before taking action.

All the work Source has put into clearing old constructs shouldn't go to waste. The reset button has already been pressed. When the moment is right, we need to embrace the new paradigm, free of old, restrictive beliefs. We can all move on as one. But only in Divine Timing.

Right now, we're all about them and us, but does that not bring 'us' closer together, strengthening our bond?

Paul makes a good point. Have I not noticed a sense of community underneath the surface? Maybe I'm trying to force things too soon, to create something in my own time? Patience has never been one of my virtues. Perhaps that's my lesson?

Incidentally, he doesn't like the God word; it's too divisive. We are all humans being, living together on this rock of Gaia. And in such close confines, it may be better to create harmony amongst us. He prefers Source. We can all put our own impression on whatever that may be.

He's definitely given me a lot to think about. I hope we get to meet again; he's so interesting to speak with."

"6th September 2069

Having discussed Paul's theories with Jennifer and Mike, we've agreed that we need to be far more subtle. We can quietly encourage from the back as opposed to leading a charge. We're down here for what could be a very long time to come.

Through means of quiet meetings, we intend to start building a sense of community. If the leaders here don't want to hear us, we will be the ears for one another. It's not all just down to me. Each person in this bunker is just as important as the next. We will be each other's support. We don't need big, grand gatherings.

At least to start, we think a sort of buddy system is a good idea. Each person should have at least one other whom they trust and can turn to if they're struggling. Fine, we may not be able to make any dramatic changes but at least we will all have someone looking out for us.

Considering we have food, water and shelter, perhaps an understanding friend ensuring positive mental health is the next most important thing.

I'm lucky; Jennifer and Mike are my backups. We're a trio, even if the two of them are joining romantically, they won't abandon me as a friend."

Chapter 9

"8th September 2069

Wow! What a day!

I went to the chapel today, still questioning God, to be honest. But left, at least, believing in my fellow man.

We were quietly saying our own prayers when a lone voice started to sing the hymn Jerusalem. I couldn't see, but I think it was Mike.

The guards got itchy fingers, but this only gave rise to courage in others. Quick as a flash, it sounded like a whole choir was belting out lyrics pondering where religious feet may have trod. Rousing is not a strong enough word.

By the time we got to singing about bringing me my bow, the atmosphere was electric. The blood stirred in my veins, my feet more connected to the ground beneath them, my heart swelling at the call. For maybe, just maybe we can build Jerusalem here, here in this hole of despair. We can bring light into this darkness.

"You will stop this," a guard cried at the top of his lungs.

Too late mate, we had already felt its power.

"Please, let us sing, it's only a hymn," one of the braver among us pleaded, his accent revealing him to be Welsh.

"It is inciteful nationalism. You will stop or bear the consequences."

The minister ummed and ahhed. Holding out his hands, he urged calm. Things were quickly escalating. We were over-excited, stirred into action.

A female voice rang out through the chaos, "Make me a channel of your peace."

Smiling, I added my voice to hers, "Where there is hatred let me bring your love."

Gradually, all who knew the hymn joined in, urging peace and harmony through the gentle hymn.

The soldiers seemed unsure what to do. We were calling for love, the opposite of inciting hatred or dissent. Yet, there was something subversive hanging in the air.

The minister dabbed his eyes, lamenting we had no choir boys for the descant.

Astonishingly, a Jewish man produced a violin and began to play tones of such utter mournfulness that even the guards were left with tears streaming. He stood alone, reaching into our souls and playing our grief on his strings, rending sobs from our hearts.

Some of us ended on our knees, doubled over, our grief spilling onto the floor, myself included. An arm was gently laid across my shoulders. I couldn't stop though, not now I'd started; the sobs and cries kept coming.

Far off, I heard the guards calling an end to the session, disbanding us. I could no more obey them than stop my tears. Broken, I thought of my babies, my husband, my family, my friends, my home, my life – all gone. More than that, I felt the pain of everyone around me; all their losses piled on top of mine.

Men and women but no children sat nearby, similarly shattered. What have we done? Why? Why, God, why? What did we do to deserve this? And why could you not have let me die with my own precious babies? Let me go to them. This long, slow wait for death is cruel. We are not the saved, we are the forsaken. The ones who bear the guilt and pain of existence, of knowing there is far worse out there that is beyond our reach.

Choked by pain, mucus and tears, I coughed, struggling for breath. A handkerchief was placed to my cheek which I automatically held in place.

"Shh now, breathe," a voice whispered across the chasm.

I tried but failed. Instead, a wail erupted.

My head was gently brought to rest against a chest.

"Back away," I heard the voice command, the reverberations trembling through me.

I don't know who he was talking to. Perhaps one of the soldiers.

Time disappeared as surely as my world.

"It's OK, I've got you," that reassuring voice told me, the arms holding me tighter, rocking me gently.

Through the blur, I made out army fatigues. It dawned on me that it was Fetu who had come to my aid once more. The realisation only brought another raft of tears, these ones in gratitude for my rescuer.

"She has to leave," someone said.

"For God's sake, look at her. Let her have a minute."

"We have our orders."

"And they will be obeyed."

"What gives? You got feelings for this one?"

"Have you not? Show some compassion. This is holy ground. She's clearly in distress."

"But – "

"We are here to protect them too, otherwise there's nothing left worth saving."

"We need to clear the area."

"Fine."

His lips close to my ear, Fetu whispered, "Put your hands around my neck."

As soon as I did, he stood with me in his arms.

"I need a medic in pursuit. Shouldn't be too hard to find one around here," he said, striding out.

My sobs softened, but salty trails still ran down my cheeks as I nestled into the strong embrace. Awkwardly, I wiped at my eyes and nose.

Back at my room, he laid me on my bed where I instantly curled into a foetal ball.

"You got a sedative or anything?" my brave soldier asked.

A sting in my arm and I slipped away.

When I regained consciousness, the first thing I noticed was a head resting on the bed, its body on the floor. I called Fetu's name and the head shot up.

"You're awake," he murmured.

He handed me a drink of water and a cereal bar. I didn't feel like eating, but he encouraged me until I took a bite.

"I need some happiness," I told him, my voice still like gravel.

Looking directly into my eyes, he slowly pulled himself onto the bed next to me, lying face up.

"Me too," he confessed.

Reaching my arm across him, I pulled myself closer.

His hand rubbed my shoulder, his lips kissed my forehead.

I looked up into sad, brown eyes and knew I would do anything to take that pain away.

Inching up his strong body, my lips found his. He kissed me back. My tongue dived into his mouth, seeking comfort, solace and kindness. That need consumed me as his arms wrapped around me like a security blanket.

His fingers ran through my hair, pulling strands off my face.

Rolling onto my back, I kicked off my scrubs.

"You're sure?" he asked on a whisper.

I nodded.

In the dull light of my room, his muscular body glinted as it was slowly released from his uniform. Chiselled grooves and peaks rippled as he moved back towards me. The man was a finely trained machine of war. But all that was coming off from him now was pure lust.

Easing himself on top of me slowly as if afraid of hurting me, he left a trail of kisses along my lips, cheeks and neck. His large hand massaged my breast before travelling down my stomach.

I came apart as his fingers felt along my labia, gliding under, between and up.

With measured care, he entered my body. My fingers clung onto his shoulders, scratched down his back as I latched on. Onto hope? Onto love? Whatever it was, I needed it and more.

Inhaling deeply at my neck, he whispered my name. Never before has 'Rachel' sounded so sweet, so desired, so needed.

Our bodies languorously moved together, absorbing every ounce of tenderness.

It was as if my soul had been sleeping and he woke me up with his spell. His mouth sucked and nipped every inch of my exposed skin.

He transported me to a dark, starless night sky, where we lit a trail of stars in our wake.

My breath dragged in like someone surfacing from underwater as a surge took over, my back arching my hips into him.

But he was relentless, offering more, and I took it. I took it all.

Grabbing handfuls of his firm buttocks, I pulled him further in, writhing in my need.

His tongue lapped mine, his fingers on the side of my face holding me.

Gathering speed and intensity, he thrust himself in and out in entrancing rhythm.

Sweat beaded on us both as we intertwined body and soul.

My hips bucked. I needed him more than oxygen.

The heat built, my muscles clenched…and then we sailed across the moon. A shining beacon blessing our union.

Exhausted, we laid on our backs, trying to regain our breath.

When I could move again, I snuggled against his chest. One arm and leg draped over him whilst his arm held me close. Another kiss landed on the top of my head.

Contentment warmed my entire being as I fell asleep in my safe, happy place.

I woke up alone in the dark. Afraid Fetu had got what he wanted and scarpered, I ran to my door.

Peering out, I saw a different guard on duty who immediately enquired why I was out of bed. I told her how I'd been sedated and woke up thinking I heard a noise. She told me to go back to bed, that all was quiet out there.

Feeling stupid, I complied. Of course, Fetu had to go when his shift ended. I hope he hadn't been discovered in my room.

Crossing back to my bed, I saw a faint glow on my table, shining from underneath my towel. Moving it, I saw a small heart shape drawn in toothpaste, a low light torch showing its location. Grinning, I mopped away the romantic gesture. The torch is being used to light my page under my covers as I write this.

Sleep eludes me, and I wanted to get all of this written before I could forget anything.

Remorse is nagging at me now. It feels like I cheated on Theo. I know he is dead and has been for months. But to jump into bed with another man so soon?

I offer up silent prayers to his soul, apologising for my actions, asking for his forgiveness and understanding. This is not normal life and I am not myself. It's as if we're living in a skewed reality, and it's one where precious little sympathy is shown.

Was it selfish of me to welcome Fetu's attentions, to latch onto the brief reprieve from the insanity? I may be losing my mind. It's all so surreal.

Conditions are harsh and very much in keeping with military life. Rigid formality reigns.

Someone please tell me this interlude from hostility was OK.

It's been an eventful day, but one that's also reminded me of the strength of humans and that love is still present despite all else."

"Aww, I'm so glad she found Fetu," Aroha said.

"Yeah, and got happy," Gerald said, signing air quotes and wiggling his eyebrows.

"Does anyone think she shouldn't have done that?" Rongo asked.

Lots of head shakes.

"Why shouldn't she?" Aroha asked with a shrug.

"We tend to be a bit more open-minded when it comes to lovemaking. In the Before, married people were promised only to one another. To be intimate with another would have been seen as a terrible betrayal."

"But it's an expression of love."

"Yes, but you were supposed to only love one person."

"Uh?"

"You could love friends and family, of course. But romantic love was reserved usually for just one person. Marriage was a promise only to be with that person for the rest of your life."

Gasps sounded amongst the teens.

"What, forever?" was asked by a few.

"Yep. I wonder what they'd think of the way we express love. Our own marriage partners are the parents of our children and have a strong bond. But nor does it limit us. Love is love and we're free to feel and demonstrate it. But then again, fertility was higher and perhaps they worried about too many children."

Discussion time followed. The class were encouraged to explore any issues which had arisen and to think about the differences in their lives.

As usual, they then gave thanks to their ancestors and to Gaia.

"Wow, intense class, huh?" Gerald asked as he walked Aroha home.

"You can say that again."

"Wow, intense class, huh?" he repeated, laughing.

"Oh wow, did you just..?" she said, giggling at his corny joke.

"Seriously though, it was_"

"Intense?" she asked back, grinning.

Playfully, he pushed her shoulder. "Stop. You know what I mean."

"Seriously though, isn't it sad that even her moment of expressing love was tinged with sadness?"

"Yeah. There was so little joy in her life."

"I hope there was some in the Before."

A frown crept along Gerald's brow. "Sadly, I don't know how there could have been."

"That's very pessimistic. I know they had very different lives, but they must've been happy sometimes."

"Maybe. In their own way," he said, shrugging.

"Makes you feel lucky, huh?"

"Defo. When you see how much more they had, so much food and stuff, it's easy to be a bit envious. But then I look around at the Talking Sessions and realise we're so much better off. We have all we need."

Stopping at her door, Aroha rubbed one foot along the back of her other leg. "I'm...I'm glad we have each other. The community, I mean."

Holding his breath, Gerald leaned forwards. His lips met hers in one delicious moment of soft warmth.

"I'm glad we have each other too," he whispered, pulling away, his eyes glimmering.

Stepping forwards, Aroha kissed Gerald's cheek before disappearing into her house.

Chapter 10

Gerald's head jerked up as Aroha entered the atrium the next morning. Smiling, she gave a single nod in his direction.

It was the hottest day yet, making it very hard going as they walked to the reading house. Thankfully, Rongo had ensured there was extra water today, which her class gulped down.

"9th September 2069

Today had been frustrating. Fetu was nowhere to be seen, and the stronger military presence made it very uncomfortable. They were out in force. I suppose a few songs have the leaders worried.

Fetu isn't my own personal bodyguard, but his presence was sorely missed. I didn't feel safe. Is this who I am now? An afraid, meek woman?

It could be pure paranoia, but eyes were on me at every turn. Avoiding any conversation, I gave the slightest nod to people I know as we crossed paths. I went to Green Space, hoping to find some peace there. But even this was denied me. I don't know what they think will happen. What can any of us do? And yesterday was none of my doing.

I've never been so pleased to see Fetu as when he snuck into my room after lights out. I'd spent all evening in there, alone, not daring to so much as poke my head out the door.

Sidling up to him, I asked, "Is that a torch in your pocket or are you just happy to see me."

Looking back, it was childish and stupid. I had actually slid his torch into his pocket as I spoke. He didn't even so much as smile. Instead, he asked me if my diary was safe. After getting over the shock of him even knowing of its existence, and asking him a million questions, I confirmed it was in its usual place.

"Is there anything about me in it, or what we did?" he asked.

I told him that of course there was.

Turns out that between him and the cleaner, they've been hiding my diary when I've been away from my room. Apparently, a false bottom to my bag was a really obvious hiding place; not my proudest moment.

Fetu has told me to check my pillow tomorrow evening, as a special one will be delivered. One with a sealed section in the middle as a new hiding place. As tensions escalate, new precautions are necessary.

Tentatively, he urged me to be wary of Jennifer and Mike. I refused to believe him when he said they're behaving suspiciously. They're my friends.

When he pointed out it was Mike who sang out first, I defended him. He was making a stand. How stupid did I feel when Fetu then highlighted how the man was left standing. "He should've got a faceful of dirt," were his precise words.

A cold stone hit my stomach. I'm pretty sure my mouth was wide open.

Yes, I would expect Mike to have been punished somehow for such behaviour. Have I not seen others battered and bruised for misdeeds? The violin player was walking with a limp as I passed him earlier. Mike was not.

Images of those furtive glances I thought were romantic between Mike and Jennifer? Were they not usually exchanged when we'd discussed some sort of theory for future plans? How could I have been so blind? No. I couldn't.

Was Fetu being honest here? He was the one snooping around my room. Is he using sex as a weapon? Getting close to me, gaining my trust just to turn me against my friends?

Honestly? I don't know what to think right now. It could look bad for any of them. Or it could look good. Perspective is everything.

I've been mulling it over. I don't have enough data. I'll just have to make my own observations and draw my own conclusions."

"Oh my gosh, she was betrayed?" Aroha gasped.

"Looks like it. But who by? Now, that is the question," Rongo answered.

The class discussed the evidence so far, who they would trust in that situation. It was roughly a fifty/fifty split. But whichever side their doubt fell on, they all agreed they felt terrible for Dr. Rachel.

"16th September 2069

It's been a week. I've tried my best to appear normal, but I'm going crazy. At one point, I half-convinced myself this is all an elaborate ruse, that none of it's real; that the bunker's just one big horrendous prank or social experiment.

In my heart, I know that's ridiculous. It'd be easier to accept than the truth though.

Jennifer took me to the gym earlier in the week, convincing me the endorphins would lift my spirits. She's been worried about me. I wish that were true.

When I got back to my room, I studied my meagre possessions. I had carefully placed everything before going out. Things had been moved.

My diary was in my pillow, I don't think that had been disturbed; it hadn't been opened, at least.

I had placed one of my blonde hairs between pages in such a way that it would have dropped out as soon as anyone read the book. At last, a practical use for it!

If Fetu had been in my room, surely, he would have gone straight to my diary? Only someone who didn't know its new location would leave it untouched. And what else would they be looking for?

The timing was uncanny too. Jennifer just happened to suggest that time to exercise? She's becoming distant. Before, I thought it was because she and Mike were getting further into a relationship. Now? I don't know. I still hesitate to cast doubt.

But what am I doing? I'm writing all this down. I'm confessing these terrible thoughts when either party could read them. But I have to tell someone, and right now, this notebook diary seems my only safe place to vent.

Chapel wasn't much help yesterday either. Everyone was tense; guards and worshippers both. The inter-faith minister announced we had a list of approved religious songs we could sing. So much for freedom to worship. It's gone the same way as freedom of speech down here.

None of the old rules seem to apply. We can all harp on about rights, amendments and constitutions, but at the end of the day, we're all expatriated. Even the Kiwis aren't truly living in New Zealand anymore.

We are Bunkerites; people with no country. All we know is Bunker.

17th September 2069

I forgot to mark it last week – we've been here six months. It should maybe hold more significance than it does. There's still at least four and a half years to go. Nothing much has changed since day 1.

Fetu was on the night shift last night and risked coming in. He's been keeping his distance all week. I think he appreciates I need the space to work this out on my own.

But he came in to let me know Mike came into my room. His colleague was on watch and pretended to walk off like he was going on patrol. But he hid until he heard one door closing and another opening. He witnessed Mike entering my room. Leaving him just long enough to start looking, the soldier went in and disturbed him.

Mike asked the soldier if he knew where I was, stating he was concerned. Obviously, he was ejected from my room immediately without comment.

If I believe all this, then Jennifer and Mike are certainly working together. Maybe feeding back to the leaders any nefarious plans I may have. Talking of which, the football tournament was stopped as guards seemed too interested in those matches. It was actually just fun. Well, maybe a little learning exercise too, but mainly about fun.

I'm such an evil mastermind! I can't even organise a bit of footie for crying out loud. Stop spying on me already.

So, who told? I didn't tell Fetu about the tournament. And I never said which days the matches were going to happen in this diary. But lots of people did know, so that doesn't necessarily make Mike and Jennifer guilty. Maybe one of the farmers squealed?

Fetu did suggest I use one of my spare notebooks to copy out this diary though. That one has love hearts drawn around the rabbit's eyes. This one has one around the nose. The eyes only see the cleaned-up version, not all the truth. Enough information to satisfy any spies, but not enough to get me into serious trouble. The nose has enough in it to get me killed, and Fetu.

And therein lies my greatest argument. I know enough about Fetu to get him into serious trouble. Mike and Jennifer? Really not very much at all.

And who was it who got me back to my room safely that day in chapel? Mike was at least there, he could have scooped me up. But he didn't even approach me. It was Fetu, supposedly my warden, who came to my aid.

But, presuming I follow this through and definitely decide I can trust Fetu and not the other two, what does that prove? What does it change? They're still my neighbours, nothing can be done to improve the situation, and we still have four and a half years to go. And what then? Will we be released into the wind like dandelion seeds? Unlikely."

"Fetu could've already reported Dr. Rachel and got her into serious trouble, but she's not so he didn't," Aroha argued in the library with her friends the next morning.

"Yeah, but so could Mike and Jennifer."

"Not without getting themselves into trouble."

"No, but if they're spies then they were only doing their duty."

"So was Fetu then," Aroha defended.

"Exactly. It's his actual job to find out this stuff. We know he knew about the diary when he shouldn't. And aren't the best spies the ones who turn the innocent on each other?"

"What would you know about it?"

"Hey, I've read some of those old crime novels," Hana countered.

"That's just fiction."

"Fiction can hold truths."

"It's made up, that's why it's called fiction," Aroha rebuffed, holding out her hands.

"Alright, that's enough," the librarian warned, walking over. "Falling out over a book is simply a waste of energy."

"We were just debating who betrayed Dr. Rachel," Aroha explained.

"I heard. It's still just a book. A diary. An important one, mind you, but you'll find out soon enough. You just keep paying attention. Now get off with you, or you'll be late for today's reading."

The librarian smiled at the retreating backs of the teenagers.

"Kids. They'll learn," she mused out loud to the book stacks.

"22nd September 2069

We sang the approved hymns in chapel today. The numbers are still holding strong. We're united. But against whom? That's still a puzzle.

The violin got confiscated as soon as it was played last time. I suspect a new one will be made, just maybe not played in that venue. It's a pity. I miss music.

It's surprising how tired I still am. Before, I was used to long, arduous shifts and I'd keep going. But now I don't seem able to ever get enough rest. Maybe it's depression? A reduced intake of oxygen? Boredom? Could there be a more sinister reason; they're sedating us somehow? Or is it a happy combination of all the above? Whatever the cause, it's unnatural.

I still don't feel like myself. I'm not even sure what that should be. Who am I? My years of medical training and practice are not being utilised, and that was such a huge part of who I used to be; it was my life.

My mind keeps wandering to all that's been lost. But then what lies ahead?

Jennifer and Mike still talk with me. I cannot help feeling a distance growing between us. Whether that's from my side or theirs, I'm not sure.

23rd September 2069

Today, I went to Green Space. Having felt so down yesterday, I hoped the greenery would lift me. I need to keep on keeping on.

Paul, the hippie, was there again. He did even more for my mood than the shrubs. Such an enlightened person. He challenges my beliefs, but in such a gentle way that I'm happy to consider his views.

I confess we spoke about the situation I find myself in. Well, one of the parties at least is reporting back, so what's the harm in opening myself up to one more? Not that I'd ever think Paul is a mole.

Maybe I should be more cautious, but with him, I feel comfortable in my own skin. And it's not like I'm hatching any takeover plans. All I want to do is get through each day the best way possible.

Paul sat quietly, patiently listening as I told him of the troubled trio. Once I'd got it all out, he made me sit in silence in turn. He talked me through a meditation, clearing my mind of clutter. At its completion, he asked what my head was telling me. And then my heart. Remarkably, I saw with clarity what my answer was.

27th September 2069

I've been observing my so-called friends, armed with my new perspective. I wanted to check that my revelation was sound.

After lights-out, I cracked my door open. Checking Fetu was still on duty, I beckoned him in. Concern was etched on his brow, and he asked if I was OK. His reaction told me everything I needed to know, should I have needed any reassurance.

I apologised, sorry for ever doubting him. I kissed and hugged him, and he returned my affection.

"It's been killing me not being able to hold you," he whispered.

"I'm so sorry," I said between kisses.

"As much as I respected your requirement for time to think, it was restrictive."

"So sorry." Kiss.

"It's not your fault. I'm sorry. I should've told you better."

143

His mouth was at my neck, his breathing ragged.

We didn't get as far as the bed. He took me up against the wall. Our need for one another equal in its intensity.

He had to return to his post immediately. Once more I was left alone and bereft.

Can I call this love? I barely know him. But it feels more than pure lust. Sure, he is smoking hot with bulging muscles and a kind smile. But it's definitely more than that. I've glimpsed the man and want to explore further. If only we could spend more time together.

1st October 2069

Fetu told me last night that I should stay back sick from breakfast this morning. Fearful something awful would happen there, I complied. A medic was sent immediately who said she'd get some mint tea sent to my room for my unsettled stomach. The room service was alarmingly swift. Some crackers arrived with the tea. They got devoured immediately.

Then the cleaner showed up. Her brown eyes were sparkling as she grinned her hello. We'd never met before, and she was excited to do so. It seems I'm getting something of a reputation. Her name is Maria. I think she's from Mexico judging by her looks and accent, but I didn't get the chance to ask.

"I have a special item today," she told me, grinning whilst pushing her laundry cart in and shutting the door.

Imagine my surprise when Fetu jumped out from beneath the towels. We were all laughing. I couldn't believe it. He was taking a huge risk, but it was such a wonderful surprise.

Maria left ASAP, leaving Fetu and me an entire day alone together. Yes, we made love, but then spent the rest of our time wrapped in each other's arms, talking.

There's only so much I should write. He was born in Samoa, but his army career has taken him to all sorts of interesting places. His eyes light up when he talks about them. He knows so much and is clearly extremely brave.

His face falls and he has puppy dog eyes when he's sad. Talking of his lost family is a sore point for him too. But we did talk about them. He had one brother and two sisters before. His parents were still married. He'd never been married himself, unwilling to leave a wife and kids alone for long periods whilst he was on active service.

He asked about my family, interested in hearing more about my children and what my husband had been like, not in a prying way. He accepts they were a part of my life and feels we should honour their memory.

We took some quiet time. Kneeling on the floor, we prayed for our loved ones and he taught me about honouring our ancestors. So many have lived before us, each contributing to our life journey. He hesitated when he said about how we contribute in our turn. I couldn't stop the tears which fell. He didn't stifle them, but merely held me in his arms whilst I got through the pain.

Fetu then explained it wasn't always through our children that we affect the lives of others. That, without realising it, I was making a difference in the bunker.

He has heard tales of others who have been inspired to set up a friendship network. My idea is spreading all across the bunker. I mean, I'd hoped it would but never really expected it to.

We discussed a warning system. Knowing Maria at least was on our side, I'd asked if other cleaners were. I don't want to detail precisely, but by folding towels and placing items a certain way, we send signals e.g. if we're under close surveillance, if it's safe etc. Fetu is going to circulate the instructions.

Like all good things, it had to come to an end. But what an amazing day."

Chapter 11

After dinner, Gerald approached Aroha.

"Seems fitting we visit our own Green Space, don't you think?" he asked from beneath his lowered lashes.

"I'd say we owe it to Dr. Rachel," she replied coyly.

There were lots of others walking around. It was always busy here, and now Aroha understood more as to the reasons why.

"It's weird to think there used to be huge expanses of green isn't it?"

"Yeah, forests of trees for miles? I know there are pictures in the nature history books, but it's still hard to imagine."

"It's sad it all went. At least, I think it did. Do you think there are forests anywhere now?"

Facing her, Gerald wrapped his arms around Aroha's waist. "I think there must be. Nature has a way of working things out. Seems to me, the problem was how many humans were cutting down loads of trees. Some even set fires on purpose. So, without all of them then maybe there are actually more trees somewhere? Free to grow without us."

"We still cut them down," Aroha said, looking down.

"Only responsibly. We replace all that we take, you know that."

"No, you're right. It just suddenly feels wrong."

Gerald kissed the top of her head. "Hey, where's this coming from? We respect Gaia. We're not like them, Aroha."

"I hope not."

"Come on. What's our motto?"

"Honesty, Respect, Fortitude."

"And do we not live by those words? Do we not honour our environment as well as each other? Is there not respect in every thought, deed and action?"

"Yeah, but...OK, I'm being silly, I'm sorry."

"No, never silly. Thoughtful and caring, just the way I like you."

His head dipped and he left a chaste kiss on her lips.

"Thank you for understanding," she murmured, snuggling against his chest in a hug.

"Always."

Hand-in-hand, they continued walking around the plants, breathing in the musty, green scent. They were mindful at first for each other's need for quiet contemplation, strolling in silence. But after a while, they diverted their attention by discussing trivial, daily matters.

Their hands were still united as they walked back home through the glass-covered corridors.

"I can't..." Gerald muttered, pulling Aroha into a quiet area.

"What?"

"I can't carry on another step without kissing you," he said, eyes glimmering, his cheeky grin spreading across his cheeks.

"What you waiting for then?" she encouraged, wrapping her hands around his neck.

His mouth racing towards hers, Gerald wasted no time in claiming the permitted kiss.

Aroha welcomed his soft, warm lips on hers. It got a bit wet as their mouths opened and closed together. Their bodies drew closer and closer as the kiss deepened. It was like someone had hooked Aroha up to a solar panel – her body buzzed and burned.

"Wow," Gerald exclaimed, breaking away first.

Aroha's mouth hung open.

"You alright?" he checked.

Blinking a few times, she found her voice. "Yeah, I think so. That was…it was…"

"Awesome."

"Yeah." A frown crossed her brow.

"Honesty, Respect, Fortitude," he reminded Aroha, catching her gaze.

"Yeah, no, it was. I'm just…a bit surprised, I guess."

Gerald's hand reached for hers. "Hey, I'm sorry."

"No, not in a bad way." Her hand went to her head.

"It wasn't awful then?" His mirthful glimmer was back.

"No, it was wonderful." She pecked his cheek.

"Phew! You had me worried a minute there."

"Maybe we should do it again, just to make sure."

Chuckling, Gerald leaned in but approaching footsteps stopped him. Holding their breath, they waited to see if the person was going to continue around the corner or come into their quiet space. They sighed out together when it turned out to be the former. But they didn't move.

Sighing, Aroha admitted, "Maybe we should just head back?"

"We're not doing anything wrong though."

"No, but I don't think I'm ready for witnesses either."

"Fair point. Come on then," he said, butting shoulders before stepping onwards.

Anyone looking couldn't be mistaken at the gathering closeness of the pairing; they were both beaming, swinging their joined hands and casting furtive glances at one another the rest of the way home.

"2nd October 2069

What do they say about crying wolf? I actually did vomit this morning.

A medic escorted me back to my room and has been asking questions.

Time meaning less here, I hadn't even counted, but my period is actually late. He's gone off to get a pregnancy test. Shit!

3rd October 2069

Hi, this is Fetu. It's a huge invasion of privacy, but I'm writing a quick entry in this diary. Sorry, Rachel.

So, why am I in possession of her most treasured item? I grabbed it as soon as the medics took Rachel away.

It was instant evac; pregnant, gone. No chance to say...congratulations? Commiserations? I don't even know how she feels about the news.

Safe to say I'm the father. She wrote such graphic detail of our encounters, I'm pretty sure she'd do likewise of any others. And did she mention the L-word?

I'm stoked that this awesome woman is even considering she has deep feelings for me.

Rachel is so much stronger than she gives herself credit for and so clever and brave and, well, she's awesome. And now she's carrying my child!

She's been taken to the family zone. It was set up for this sort of scenario. A few children were brought along initially.

It was seen as a good idea to keep them separate though, as the families who had been separated would feel jealous and it may cause friction. Yeah, I bet it would. Rachel is gonna be pissed when she discovers that!

I wish I'd warned her. The kids there, they have the favoured genes. No, there would never be a right way of telling her. It's like saying her kids weren't worthy and that's just wrong, total bullshit. This knowledge makes me sick. I wish I'd never found out. But it's what made me want to actively help the people here, to go beyond my duty.

Rachel, when you read this, I'm so sorry. Please forgive me. Thank you. I love you.

Trust me when I say I don't know who our leaders are. I know you're anxious to find out. My instructions come through the ranks. My duty was to obey. I'm a military man. You, Rachel, helped open my eyes, to make me question what was previously unquestionable. I am grateful to you for that and so much more.

Until my dying breath, I will protect you and our child."

"Oh my gosh," Aroha gasped along with her classmates.

"What the frick?" Gerald added.

Allowing the class to absorb the shock, Rongo waited before she said, "Alright. I know this is a harsh truth. What are we all feeling?"

Many questions were asked as the class tried to understand how and why people would be treated that way.

"Well, I guess now we know Fetu was on Dr. Rachel's side," Aroha wondered out loud.

"You reckon?" Rongo queried.

"No, don't tell me he's not. Not now."

"We'll have to find out."

"Rongo, no, don't do this to me. He's good, I know he is."

"Only time will tell. But I think we've had enough for today."

Amidst protestations, Rongo closed the session.

Everyone chattered on the way back, offering theories and exchanging opinions.

Once they were back at the atrium, Aroha led Gerald away, making their way home on their own.

"Gerald…I…I think I want you to be my first," she stuttered.

Pulling on her hand, he brought her to a stop so he could kiss her.

"Aroha, it would be my honour. But only once that 'think' is a 'know', OK?"

She nodded.

"But you should know, I'm already protective over you. If I had my way, I'd be your first and your last."

"I think I know that. Maybe that's why I've been hesitating. I don't know if I can promise that."

"I'm not asking you to. I know it's old fashioned. That sort of thinking belongs in the Before. I can't explain it. But when I saw Charles looking at you that way, it triggered something in me, a protective instinct, I dunno what to call it."

"Thank you for your honesty."

"Always."

Aroha guided his head to hers and took control of the next kiss. This one was deeper and more sensual.

With a sharp intake of breath, Gerald broke away. "When it's an I know, Aroha."

"OK."

"10th of the 10th 2069

It feels like an auspicious day when written like that.

Yes, Fetu has managed to get my diary back to me now. It took a few days, but it's here. I read his addition. I've got mixed feelings about it. But mostly I'm happy to hear from him. He loves me! Wow! Knowing him better now, I think I have to say I share the sentiment, for all the good it does us.

He's not able to get this far into the bunker, and it's like he's miles away. Once more I'm ripped away from the father of my child.

How odd that still sounds. How the hell did I end up pregnant? Spare me, I'm a doctor, I know the biology. It's just I'm amazed at how twisted fate is.

The father of my child...that used to be Theo's privilege. And now it's someone else. I never ever would have thought that possible. But here I am.

Of course, I've not told anyone who the father is. They have their suspicions, but I'm not about to confirm them. I've no idea what they'd do to him. There will probably be DNA tests, given what Fetu mentioned. They can work it out themselves. I owe them nothing.

There are children here. The bastards brought children, families into the bunker but not mine. Damn right I'm angry. Who the hell are they to judge my own flesh and blood not worthy of saving but these kids are? How dare they? Who does that? Sick, sick bastards!

I wonder who these children are. Are any of them related to the elusive leaders? No, they're probably in their own privileged bunker elsewhere. And I can't hate these innocents, these victims of disaster. It wasn't their choice any more than it was mine.

Would I not have jumped at the chance to bring my own family? I can't blame the parents. I doubt they had much say in the matter either, anyway. None of us did.

But what's to happen to me? The future of humanity is spewed as a phrase, so I hope they won't reject my own child. And so far, they're taking care of me, to the point of fussing.

I've been assigned what's laughably called a midwife. Nanny seems more appropriate. Her name's Becky and she has blonde hair and blue eyes like me. She's from Germany and is actually very sweet. Honestly? She's simply overjoyed at having a job again. I'm sure I'd be over-enthusiastic if anyone needed an oncologist right now.

And I'm ever so grateful to her as she reunited me with my diary and has pledged to help me hide it. It seems I need to trust her. I suppose, after recent events, my trust in others is somewhat shaken. But that's not Becky's fault. And it's nice to have a friend. We share a room so she may tend to my every need. Give me strength!? But it's good to have company.

There was a short note provided, letting me know the decoy has disappeared. Thank goodness I wrote it!

I can't say I'm sorry at being removed from Jennifer and Mike. It's increasingly likely they were spies. How low can people get? I'm so hurt by their betrayal.

The people I had to put my faith and trust in abused it in the cruellest way imaginable at the worst possible time.

Becky's feeding me supplements such as nut-based paste as though I were starving. I'm sure I'm not malnourished, at least not to the extent I require such treatment. However, they insist that it's for the good of the baby. Who am I to turn down extra food? And if they're that concerned, it's a good sign they'll let me go full term.

But woe betide anyone if they try to take my baby away once it's born. NOT GOING TO HAPPEN!"

"Oh, poor Dr. Rachel," Hana droned.

Others murmured agreement.

"It's just too terrible. Haven't they hurt her enough? How many loved ones can she be torn from?" Aroha asked.

"It does seem extreme. Perhaps we'll discover the reasoning as we move forwards? We've already heard they were protective of the children, fearing envy from those without their families," Rongo said.

"Is it so different?" one boy asked.

"Are you serious?" Aroha shot back.

"Don't we have a special area for expectant mothers?"

"Not like that, not in isolation of everyone else. Our nursery is there to support not hide. And people are free to come and go. I can't believe you even said that," Aroha said, fire shooting from her eyes.

"I was only asking."

"Quite. Aroha, we don't criticise questions."

"Sorry, Rongo," she apologised, looking at the ground. "I didn't mean...it's just...I'm so cross for Dr. Rachel."

"Your anger and shock are understandable. But don't take it out on others here. It's not them you're angry with."

"Sorry, Harry."

"Accepted. It is bad, what they did. I didn't mean we're like that. I was just trying to understand why they did it."

"Now that's settled, shall we continue?" Rongo asked.

"12th October 2069

When Becky and I returned from breakfast, I noticed my towel had been placed askew. Nudging it, a toothpaste heart was revealed.

My own heart leapt into my mouth. Was he here? No, not even he could manage that. It must've been the cleaner relaying his message.

Aww. I will have to try to relay one back. I daren't send a written note. I'll try and think of a suitable object signal for tomorrow morning.

I've written a lot of information. I really hope Becky is truly dependable.

Becky, if you're reading this, I'm so sorry. I don't mean to doubt you. I hope you understand it's others who have hurt me and caused this irrational fear.

20th October 2069

Heck, has it been over two weeks already? We have more light in this section. Everything feels brighter and fresher. It's odd, despite being pregnant which usually makes me sleepy, I'm more alert than I've been in ages.

We even have our own Green Space, which I'm calling Green Space 2; original, eh? I've visited the park there where children play. Their laughter fills my heart with joy. How I've missed that sound. But it punches my gut at the same time, reminding me of Joshua and Ella. If I don't keep saying their names I'm scared I'll forget them. And Theo, of course.

I'm constantly monitored with machines and tests. It seems electricity is prioritised here; nothing is spared. I suppose it makes sense when this will become a vital hub for breeding more of our species.

It's all so surreal! What the hell did I just write? I talk of humans as being endangered. How on Earth did it come to this?

A couple of other pregnant mums are here too. None of us are sharing the daddy's names. Deeksha is from India and was a teacher before. Her long, black hair is to die for; it's so shiny and lush.

Emma was an American construction engineer and has light brown hair and green eyes. They're both very pretty.

It's a wonder we don't have more expectant mums; I think I noted before how we all seem to have been selected for looks as well as skills. In close confines? Come on, people, what else is going to happen with nothing else to do, no matter how much you segregate us?

Just as I was getting to know Fetu better, we've been separated. It's annoying as much as unjust. Stupid fertile me. Trust me to get pregnant straight away. I wasn't thinking, and it's not like contraception's available even if I hadn't been acting on sheer instinct. What's done is done though.

I wonder if Joshua and Ella would mind having a little brother or sister?

Anyway, Deeksha, Emma and I are bonding, brought together by circumstance. It's fascinating hearing all about their former lives.

Deeksha was a mum before too, so shares my mixed emotions. She perhaps feels even more guilty, considering her stricter upbringing. It's an odd but great comfort to have someone who truly understands.

Poor Emma is expecting her first child, so is full of nerves, more so for this strange environment we find ourselves in. But we're supporting her as best we can.

They each have a midwife too. There are times when just we mums are together, and I think the midwives congregate somewhere else. I'm sure we're all swapping notes. We're in danger of becoming the proverbial mother hens!

We have our own chapel here too. A different inter-faith minister presides. It's mainly women and children, but there's a few single dads. It's weird. It feels so forced/contrived. But it's what we have. And I'm attending, praying to the God I hope exists that He'll keep my baby safe and with me, as well as protecting the souls of my previous family. Not that I ask for much, eh?

I'm starting a new family! It's all wrong."

"I can't believe Dr. Rachel got pregnant first go," Aroha said as she and Gerald walked home.

"Pretty incredible, huh?"

"Today, I'd say she was lucky. Then? Maybe unlucky. But then it got her out of the medic zone and into somewhere friendlier."

"It's hard to know how to feel. Like Rongo said, conflicted seems to cover it."

"You don't think I'll get pregnant straight away, do you?"

Gerald's laugh was a nervous one. "Highly unlikely. But I guess you never know."

Aroha went silent. Just as she thought she was ready to lie with Gerald, this comes up. She'd not even started her full medic training yet. She wanted to be doing her life's work before she became a mum. Was it worth the risk? Other people did it. But what if she waited too long, and then she never became a mum?

Chapter 12

"31st October 2069

Today would be Halloween. Not that we can really do anything to celebrate it now. Besides, we have no harvest to be thankful for and keep safe. This is something which had increasingly been celebrated at home – precious food.

Reality here is scarier than any costume or ghost story. Trapped in an underground cave system for years, that's the stuff of horror stories, right?

My hormones are all over the place. I'm excited one minute, down the next. OK, I'm going to stop writing now.

9th November

Diwali starts today for our Indian Bunkerites. We gathered in chapel and lit candles. And there were some sweet treats at dinner. Again, the lack of fireworks was commented on – it seems they were a big part of many cultures and are sorely missed. There were certainly no Guy Fawkes events on the 5th November.

Anyway, we celebrated Diwali together as much as we could.

11th of the 11th

Armistice Day.

We had a special service in the chapel today. We used to mourn the fallen in battle and think the numbers were high. We knew nothing. Presumably, most of the human race has now been eradicated by war, the likes of which were inconceivable. Not just soldiers. Billions of fatalities as opposed to millions. It's insane.

151 years since the cessation of hostilities in World War I, and here we sit in the ruins of World War III.

I think it's really hit home today that this little life growing inside me really may be one of the Chosen; he/she will become responsible for the future of mankind. I sort of knew, but now I KNOW. Does that make sense? The weight of the world is bearing down on me. The responsibility is terrifying. This is our future. I am carrying a rare human. This is it.

Who would have thought this could be possible? It's ridiculous. Unfathomable. But it's real, isn't it? Oh God, it's real.

20th November 2069

The paternity tests have been done. The results are in. I pray Fetu is safe and they've not done anything dreadful to him.

There is a tiny ray of hope that they'll bring him to me, that the leaders want to encourage families. But so long as he's alive and well, I shall be happy.

28th November 2069

Because there are so many Americans down here, today we had a Thanksgiving feast. By feast I mean we had a little bit of roast chicken and vegetables.

I've not learned whether we have livestock; I think we do. These precious chickens were probably fresh. Freezers to contain enough food for us all would take too much electricity, I think. Although, I do suspect we have some.

What do the animals eat though? Is it possible to store enough grain for chickens? Are there cows, pigs or sheep too? I'd not managed to get that information from the farmers – there always seemed to be other things to discuss.

We had a special sermon, encouraging us to count our blessings. We are survivors with shelter, food and health – so much better off than so many outside, I suspect.

And, there's new life within me. I am thankful for the kindness and affection of Fetu. I pray he is safe, that the leaders haven't had him executed for going against orders.

1st December 2069

My prayers today have been answered. I fell to the floor weeping as we returned to our room after chapel today. There was a toothpaste heart under my towel. He's safe. Praise the Lord, Fetu is well. Poor Becky wondered what on earth had come over me at first.

She's so good. She held me, waiting for my sobs to recede far enough for an explanation to be provided.

As soon as I recovered, I went in search of Deeksha and Emma to tell them. They've not heard anything from their partners, but surely this gives us all hope.

5th December 2069

Well, it doesn't seem like Fetu is allowed to come and live with me; I'm too afraid to ask in fear of further jeopardising our precarious position. But at least he's safe. I shall have to be satisfied with that. I am. I'm happy. It could have been far worse. But there are other families here. Why is he not allowed to join me?

8th December 2069

Hannukah (I think that's how you spell it) started today. Like Diwali, we had a ceremony in chapel where we were all encouraged to take part. The first candle was lit on the menorah. I'm so sorry, I've not celebrated this before. I'm not sure if I'm recording these correctly.

There were some fried dishes at dinner which were super tasty.

A new candle is lit each night for 8 nights. It is a festival of lights.

In trying to learn and join in with others for their celebrations, it strikes me that there are similarities. Christmas, which some say used to be Yule - a celebration of the return of the sun, is about the birth of Christ the saviour – often depicted with a shining halo. It falls near the shortest day of the year in the UK.

So, lights are important to us all. Illuminating this dark period.

25th December 2069

It's the best Christmas ever! Fetu was permitted a visit today. We weren't left alone, of course, but we didn't care. Our hands were all over each other, trying to check we were real, needing reassurance through touch. Kisses were trailed across cheeks, mouths, arms, hands; everywhere. Tears poured from our eyes. Our hug rivalled bears in ferocity and strength.

As if realising how tightly he was squeezing, Fetu stepped back, his hands on my little bump.

"You're well?" he asked.

"Yes, yes, I'm well. And you? They didn't hurt you?"

His eyes left mine as he glanced away and down.

"Good God, what did they do?"

"It's nothing, I'm alright," he whispered.

My hands cupped his face. "Truly?"

"I'm OK," he confirmed before kissing me fully.

"Better for seeing you," he told me after the best kiss of my life, his voice hoarse.

We were ushered to chapel, where we sang Christmas carols and remembered the birth of Jesus Christ. My hand stroked my belly. *Giving birth here is nothing compared to being in a stable. I can do this.*

I was overjoyed to see Deeksha and Emma with their partners too. Theirs are not soldiers but inmates, civilian men from their zone. The relief at reuniting is the same though.

After the service, we went to the dining hall which had a few decorations hanging up. Another little roast chicken meal was laid out for us.

Best of all was a Christmas pudding. There must be an English chef or leader somewhere to even think of cooking that. And it was the best tasting food ever to pass my lips. Fetu joked at the orgasmic sounds coming from me as I ate.

"Why can't he stay?" I pleaded as we were told to say our goodbyes.

We'd not even had a conjugal visit. Come on, even prisoners used to get those. I'm already pregnant. And craving bodily contact. But in another perverse twist of cruelty, we were denied the pleasure. Literally!

Fetu explained he had to go, that duty called. That if they started housing all the families together, there'd be nobody left to run the place, to perform essential tasks. The time will come when people are encouraged to procreate. We just jumped the gun.

It seems he was pre-warned. Me? I was given false hope.

Like a toddler, I cried and screamed for him as he was led away, stretching out my arms towards the disappearing form of Fetu. Deeksha and Emma were likewise devastated. Our midwives crowded round us, urging calm, that such hysterics weren't good for our babies. Well, bring our lovers back – that would be good for us!

Given time alone, my mourning of Christmases lost took over. No more excited Joshua or Ella waiting for Father Christmas. No family feast. Never again will they enjoy a Christmas.

And there it arrived; the worst Christmas ever."

Having checked all the pupils were alright, and discussing the issues in these latest diary entries, Rongo clapped her hands once, loudly.

"OK, everyone. That's a great place to stop. We have no class tomorrow as Summer Solstice celebrations take precedence. This is, of course, when they would celebrate Christmas and maybe Hannukah in the Before. When we come back, I want you all to think about those festivals and how they are different and similar to ours. But for now, go and have fun. I expect to see you all dancing by the fire."

The day of Summer Solstice celebrations began, after essential chores were taken care of, in the meeting house. A special talking session was held where everyone was encouraged to offer thanks. Offerings were made to Source, in thanks for this year and requesting protection for the next. Communal wine was passed around as were small spiced biscuits.

Families went off in groups to celebrate privately in their own homes for the afternoon. Time spent together to appreciate their blood ties. Incense was burned in rituals for the family's ancestors.

Everyone got busy, draping themselves in a white wrap, akin to a toga, putting dried flowers, herbs and leaf wreaths on their heads. Excitement built as they all eagerly awaited the signal to leave.

When the sun was low enough and less harmful, strategically placed gongs sounded, struck by the leaders. Filtering out of their homes, the villagers congregated at the centre, then paraded down to the sea, carrying torches and chanting songs.

Gathering on the shore, the leaders gave a fine speech about thanking the sun for its light and warmth, formally asking for a bountiful harvest this coming year. A small bonfire was lit on the sand which threw the figures into silhouette as they removed their robes and wreaths.

En masse, the village surged forwards into the sea, squealing and yelping as their limbs sank further into the water. Some dashed straight back out, having satisfied the essentials of the ritual; washing away any negativity from the year. But others remained and even managed to swim a little. Aroha was one of the latter group.

"Aargh," she screeched at Gerald as he splashed water at her.

He just laughed as she retaliated.

Their limbs thrashed as they created ever-bigger waves over one another, only stopping when their laughter had forced all the air out of their lungs. Standing in the shallows, they drew in deep breaths, trying to stifle giggles.

Aroha caught Gerald's stare and everything stopped, silence fell like a blanket. She was suddenly aware of her nudity as his eyes roamed over her breasts.

"What?" she asked him, her hands covering her bared flesh.

"Sorry, I couldn't help myself."

"It's not like you've never seen me naked."

"I know. It's just, well, it's different now." He looked down at himself.

Aroha followed his gaze and blushed. "Oh."

His hand brushed the back of his head. "Yeah, so, that."

"Er…"

"You're beautiful, Aroha. Every part of me appreciates every part of you."

Looking away, she blushed and smiled. "Thank you. I feel the same."

"Hey," he called, wading towards her, his hand going to her cheek. "Don't be embarrassed by such a wonderful feeling."

Her brown eyes met his. "I'm not. Not really. I'm still getting used to it. I've always loved you. But it was like a friend…"

"And now?"

Her breath came out on a whispered sigh. "And now, I love you love you."

Still maintaining eye contact, he answered, "I love you too."

Their mouths drew slowly together as they drank each other in. Their kiss was languorous and soothing as much as exciting, like they were reassuring one another. Their naked bodies were touching, water dripping from them.

"We should go join the others," Aroha moaned.

"We don't have to."

"Yeah, we kinda do."

He rolled his eyes. "Yeah, I know. OK, come on then."

Reluctantly, they left the water. Finding a robe on the shore, Aroha quickly wrapped herself back up and headed closer to the fire to warm up, Gerald close on her heels. The evening air was cold, especially against her wet skin.

A wreath was placed on her head and hands were on her upper arms, rubbing vigorously.

"Thank you," she said, not even having to look behind her.

"Anytime," Gerald said, kissing close to her ear.

He sped away, leaving Aroha to mingle with the villagers who were also gathered by the fire.

"Here, get this down you," he said, nudging the cup at her as he returned.

Taking a sip of the hot, spiced cider, Aroha's eyes closed. "Mmm…that's so good."

Dipping his head, Gerald's tongue licked across her lips. "Mmmm…yeah."

Laughing, Aroha playfully shoved his shoulder. "You kook."

Some of their friends joined them then, causing a distraction with their frivolous conversations and barbecue pulled pork sammies. Laughter filled the air around them.

Drums boomed across the crowd, reverberating through every being, calling to something deep within. The villagers hushed, turning towards the sound. Hands clapped and feet stomped to the rhythm.

Dancers in grass skirts trooped out and kicked off the festivities with a haka, honouring their ancestors.

Conch shell horns sounded out at its conclusion, calling everyone to form a line. Taking a torch each, lighting it from the bonfire, the villagers assembled. Their orange glow trailed along the cliffs as they made their way up to the highest peak.

The leaders lit the large bonfire and the dancers arranged themselves in front. A few more ancestral dances ensued, with swaying hips, hand gestures, calls and chants. They were all met with hollers.

The villagers followed the dancers in a tour of the largest bonfire, all unburdening themselves of their torches, adding flames to flames.

Their headdresses were also now thrown into the fire; symbolic of more offerings and prayers but also adding a sweet fragrance.

Now free to join in the dancing, raucous celebrating erupted in full force.

Every man, woman and child danced and cheered, letting their hair down, giving thanks and embracing the longest day of the year.

Aroha was jumping up and down with the continuing beat, her body getting steadily closer to Gerald. Gyrating her hips, she edged closer still. Stretching her arms out, she placed them on his shoulders, grinding against him, demanding he echo her moves.

Together, they swayed. Together, they celebrated. Together, their lips joined.

Their mouths were also in harmony with the pulse of the music, working with one another, their tongues dancing. With hips still rolling, the pair fell into the call of the chants. All that existed was them and the rhythm.

"Alright you two, get a room," one of their friends chimed.

Breaking away, the pair nervously laughed, shrugging away any awkwardness.

They separated slightly and tried to include their friends in their celebration. But soon, they edged closer again, the music commanding their bodies without conscious thought.

Gerald tossed his head diagonally with a raised eyebrow. Reaching for his outstretched hand, Aroha followed. Down and around the brow they walked away, finding a secluded spot amongst the brush.

Aroha leaned into Gerald, regaining the kiss which had been so painfully interrupted. Her hands wandered down and held onto his buttocks through the flimsy fabric. She could feel his arousal against her stomach.

"Geez, Aroha, please tell me you know," he begged, his breathing ragged.

"I know more than anything in my life," she muttered.

"Thank Source."

His hands searched all over her body, cupping her breasts, running up and down her back. Finally, pushing her robe aside, his fingers delved between the apex of her thighs, massaging her nub until she cried out, her leg hoisted against him and head thrown back.

"Say it, Aroha."

"Gerald, I need you to be my first. Now," she whimpered.

Laying down on the ground, Aroha's legs widened, inviting Gerald in. Needing no further encouragement, he gently lowered himself on top of her. With the assistance of one hand, he found her entrance, and moved his hips forwards, tantalisingly slowly. Only stopping when Aroha cried out. But she urged him on.

Their bodies writhed, backwards and forwards. The drums a distant thrum, spurring them on.

Aroha's body burned as if licked by the flames of an inner bonfire. She thrashed at its touch, clawing the ground underneath her.

Onwards, Gerald thrust.

Powerless to resist, her hips bucked. She needed more of him.

She nipped at his neck and inhaled his scent. Her back arched as he powered on, gliding in and out, up and down. She could feel him inside her but still she wanted more. Her hands clenched his buttocks, hips rocking against his.

Wrapping her legs around his waist, Aroha clung on, inviting him ever further. Whimpers leapt from her lips which were quickly covered by his in a passing kiss.

Gerald paused. "OK?"

"Please don't stop," she begged.

He readily complied, once again finding his rhythm echoing the drums.

Heat fired through Aroha's body, her hips bucked and then she rode the waves as her muscles clenched around him, catapulting her into the sun itself. More intense than when his fingers had moved against her, she came apart around him.

Landing back to Earth with a bump, she heard his groans, crying out her name as he too found release.

Aroha wondered if she would ever want this with anyone else. Gerald had warned her of his feelings. It wasn't unheard of in their culture, but it was surprising. But the sudden strength of her own feelings was astonishing. She just wanted him.

Catching her breath, Aroha kissed Gerald's lips. A sweet modest peck, out of keeping with what they'd just done. Almost shy.

In answer, Gerald's lips dragged along hers, slower, inviting them to open, smooching.

"You're incredible," he whispered.

"Just wow," she replied breathily.

Taking a moment to hold each other, they revelled in their afterglow.

"I hate to say it—" Aroha muttered.

"I know, we should get back."

Righting their robes, they returned to the revellers, blending in with the dancing throng. Together, the village celebrated until just after dawn.

Chapter 13

The next morning was a late start for all. Hot lemon water greeted them at their simple breakfast. Everyone worked together, ensuring essential tasks were complete before having a lazy day.

Gerald went to Aroha's house with her, where they hauled up in her bedroom. Sore and exhausted, she just wanted to cuddle, and he was more than happy to provide that for her.

Waking up from a joint nap, Gerald suggested, "A group of us are meeting down on the beach later. Fancy it?"

"Mmm...sure, why not?" she said, rubbing her eyes.

Aroha had been afraid it would be awkward after their joining, that it'd somehow damage their friendship. But now she realised they were closer than ever. When they were silent, it was a comfortable peace which held them. And when they spoke, it was as if nothing had happened; the same easy conversation as always.

When they emerged from her room, they found Aroha's parents in the lounge.

"We're off to the beach," she told them.

Her mum jumped up. "I have some stuff in the brew room you can take with you."

Aroha dutifully followed her mum to the small room, designed so they could make drinks and snacks. It was akin to a small kitchen. Their main meals were always a communal affair, so they didn't need a large space in their homes.

"I'm so glad you chose Gerald. Congratulations," her mum said, kissing her cheek as she handed over a box of sweet treats.

"What? How did you—"

"I have eyes, sweetheart. For what it's worth, I think he's a wonderful boy."

"Muuuum!"

"Alright, alright, off you go."

Her mum's eyes glistened as she watched them go out the door, grinning.

They were careful to wear long sleeves, aware of the harmful UV rays of the afternoon sun.

"And what did you two get up to last night, as if we didn't know?" Hana called across to the pair as they approached along the sand.

A group of their friends circled them and chanted, congratulating Aroha and Gerald on their union. The 'first' was a big deal, and like all things, loved ones liked to celebrate such moments. Nothing escaped the community.

As soon as they reached puberty, the villagers regularly underwent sexual health checks as well as the usual health ones. And fertility rates were low. It didn't cross anyone's mind that pregnancy may be an option so soon. It was purely a joyous occasion, a celebration of love.

Charles was there, not looking quite so happy as their other friends, but managed to wish them well all the same.

Aroha produced the box of treats and others brought leftovers across.

"So, what do we make of Christmas?" Aroha asked, sitting down.

"Well, that was a Christian celebration, wasn't it? Celebrating the birth of Jesus Christ," Hana answered.

"A light to the world?" Aroha suggested with a shrug.

"Bit tenuous, but yeah, maybe," Charles agreed.

"Don't forget the other religions. They all seemed to share a celebration of light," Hana chipped in.

"But we do that more at Winter Solstice," someone else said.

"Yeah, but a lot of those religions were from the northern hemisphere, though. Their winter was our summer," Aroha noted.

"Yeah, that makes sense. So, that's kind of the same. It's like our founding members took the best bits of all those individual religions and formed a united one," Gerald pondered.

"It was kind of awkward. All those separate celebrations. There would have been too many festival days spread across so few people in each," Aroha added.

"Nobody would ever have got any work done. Everyone would have felt obliged to celebrate everything so as not to let anyone feel left out," Charles remarked.

"Haha, yeah, I suppose it made sense to amalgamate. Unite all people. But did we lose something in the process?"

"I don't know. It's all about respecting one another and loving your neighbour when you boil it all down, right?"

They fell into analysing what they knew of the religions of the world in the Before.

"And having such divisive opinions seemed to give way to wars," Hana said.

"Hm, I still don't know if that was an excuse though," Aroha replied, frowning.

"Well, I like the way we have it now. Nobody's upset with anyone. We're all different but respected and yet kinda the same," Gerald declared.

"Yeah, peace, harmony and love," Charles muttered.

Happily, their conversation fell to more general things after that. The late afternoon and early evening disappeared in the reassuring presence of friends.

Those of the group who had been at the beach and were in class the next day, put forward their thoughts as others shared theirs. Rongo congratulated them on their insights.

"Shall we see what else we can discover?" she said, segueing into the reading.

"1ˢᵗ January 2070

A new year, but no new start. Who would have thought this time last year that we'd end up here?

The girls and I are still a little subdued. They're a great support, and we're helping one another through. But as our bellies slowly expand, the walls seem to close in. What world are our children being born into? We're all praying that at least there's a chance of peace now.

12ᵗʰ January 2070

Life has settled into a routine.

Becky is making sure I'm comfortable and cared for, but it's making me feel lazy. I try to walk in Green Space 2 as much as possible.

I'm denied any research notes here. Only gentle exercise is permitted. So, when I'm not with Deeksha and Emma, reading is my main hobby. Thank goodness for a small library. Becky is trying to teach me to knit; apparently, it's a useful hobby. I think she has grand visions of us knitting blankets for the entire community.

20th January 2070

Today is my 37th birthday. Nobody seems to know, and I've not told them. It's not something that feels like it should be celebrated. My wheel of life keeps turning whilst so many others have had theirs stopped. I'm grateful to be alive. I've read back some of my entries and realise it may not seem that way, but I am.

Our partners have not repeated their visit. That was clearly just a special Christmas thing. I'd really like Fetu to be here, at least for the birth. I wonder if they'll permit that.

2nd February 2070

It's a boy!

Amidst a plethora of tests, they checked the sex of my baby. I'm expecting a boy. I've asked them to tell Fetu. Surprisingly, they said they would. I hope they're true to their word.

Becky has brought in several books of baby names. I'm going to take them to the other mums so they can help me choose the best name for my little one.

Deeksha has already found out she's expecting a girl and has decided on Aarushi. It means the first rays of the sun – a most fitting and beautiful name. Hopefully, she'll see that glowing orb one day. Until then, she'll be Deeksha's little ray of hope.

Emma has decided on not being told yet. She's getting more nervous as time passes, despite our best efforts.

7th February 2070

Under my towel today was a pair of hearts. I guess the father knows and is happy then. Gratitude swelled my heart so much that my eyes leaked!

9th February 2070

Now I know Fetu knows we're having a boy, I'm happier in making a decision as to the name of our baby.

Akamu – *ahKAAMuw*

It's Polynesian, well, maybe Hawaiian, but was supposedly popular in Samoa where Fetu was born. It means Adam, which is rather amusing given our situation. In turn, that means 'of the red earth', which he is. Born unto those living on a probably scorched planet.

It also partners quite nicely with Deeksha's Aarushi. Well, let's face it, there may not be a large choice of partners in life. And if they're both heterosexual, it's a possibility they'll be together.

And it's nothing like Ella or Joshua. That would feel wrong. I'm not replacing them. Nobody ever could. How my heart weeps still. I will never forget them. Sometimes, I think I will crumble into tiny pieces but then I think of Akamu and know I must be strong for him. This is not his fault. He deserves better.

I've given all of this way too much thought. But there's precious little to occupy myself with.

15th February 2070

Yesterday was Valentine's Day. I did have a toothpaste heart under my towel, and hopefully, Fetu found a matching one. But that was the extent of it. No visit. Why are the leaders so insistent on this ridiculous separation? They'd better not try to take my baby away!

Another expectant mum has been brought in this week. Debbie used to work in Kew Gardens; a fellow Brit. She has the most gorgeous blue eyes which contrast with her dark hair. Bless her, she was frantic at first, but thankfully, we've been able to reassure her that her lover won't be killed. I couldn't say harmed; I suspect Fetu was subjected to vicious reprimands, but then he's a soldier. I left all of that out of our conversations, obviously. We just let her know of our positive experiences.

Once she'd settled in, we got to talking. Several gardeners and horticulturists from Kew in London and The Eden Project in Cornwall are down here. Or, at least, they used to be from those places. We're all just Bunkerites now, aren't we? No other place exists. But we all still have a role.

Debbie's been looking after the plants in the Green Spaces. She let on that there's seed banks, so when we finally go back into the outside, and when the soil has been nurtured with tender loving care, we can replant many species. That must be what they're planning with crops too. Debbie's focus is on trees though. They'll surely absorb pollutants and produce oxygen; even more vital now, I imagine.

It's so strange, being literally kept in the dark. None of us knows what the state of the world is in above our heads or how catastrophic the impact may have been.

28th February 2070

Poor Debbie is experiencing terrible morning sickness. Oddly, mine wasn't as bad as my previous pregnancies. Maybe because I was forced to rest? With limited variety, Becky has done an excellent job of tailoring my diet to help too; some preserved ginger was found.

No matter how much I keep telling myself it's happening, this life is still surreal. At home, I had my successful career, a husband, two children, a nice home. I had it made! My life was on track. Happy. I'd had as many children as I was going to, and they were at school. Stop; not going there.

What I was trying to say was, I never expected to have any more children. 40 isn't that far away, and I'm pregnant, the father absent, living separately in a bizarre cave system. No house, no career, no husband.

It's been almost a year, and I still can't believe it. I keep expecting to wake up, to discover this was all just a dreadful nightmare. Or that my family will walk in through the doors.

Coming to terms with this existence? Every fibre of my being resists.

Hippie Paul's words return in times of my deepest distress, bringing comfort and hope. All we have is now.

Not living in the past, I'm living in the present. As a Bunkerite. With an uncertain future. I crave stability and hope.

12ᵗʰ MARCH 2070 – 1 YEAR

Gosh, one year. It seems an eternity. Yet the pain of separation feels as if it happened this morning.

What is happening on the surface?

Do we truly have four more years to go? Do we have enough food to even do that?

Dried goods only last so long.

I've been craving cherryade, which is remarkably in our stores. Fizzy drinks were stockpiled. Way to encourage healthy living!? But in previous scenarios, it was discovered that these were not damaged by radiation. I discovered this in the early days but have only just realised I forgot to mention it. Sorry. It's sometimes hard to decide what's important. Fizzy drinks weren't high on my agenda.

The midwives here are fans of bone broth; good thing I was never vegetarian! But presumably, some people are. Hippie Paul was possibly vegan. What's he eating? It occurred to me before, but I've not managed to find out. I kept forgetting to ask when I saw him – he always distracted me with philosophy.

Anyway, happy one year, Bunkerites!?

"How are we all? I know there was a lot to get through today," Rongo said.

"She's like the waves," Hana murmured.

"That's an interesting thought. Would you like to expand on that?"

"It's like her temper rises then dies. Her sadness floods and recedes."

"That's excellent, Hana. Yes, Dr. Rachel seems to try to battle her emotions, which causes more anger. And then, at other times, she's resigned to her situation. Have you noticed what her triggers are?"

"Her children," Aroha noted. "Her anger rises each time she writes about them."

"Yes."

"She's still grieving. I'm not sure the shock's worn off. Can it last that long, shock?"

"Well, under distressing circumstances, it probably can."

"So much sadness."

"Well, there wasn't much to be happy about, was there?" Gerald added.

"She's scared," Hana rejoined. "Dr. Rachel still doesn't know if she'll have to fight to keep the baby growing inside her. Or when she'll next see Fetu."

"Precisely. Fear is a powerful emotion which often leads to anger. And she's been kept in that emotional state for a year," Rongo replied.

"If they just showed compassion, people would be a lot happier."

"It's very unusual for us. There's a cold logic to their leaders' actions. They're trying to control the population in every way. They seem to have forgotten that people have emotions, have other basic needs apart from food and shelter."

After class, Aroha headed home. Finding her parents were still out, she invited Gerald in.

"I'm so grateful for our freedom," Aroha said as she lounged against her boyfriend on her bed.

"I'm grateful for you," Gerald said, leaning down to kiss the top of her head.

"I don't know what I'd do if anyone tried to separate us."

"Shh, don't even think about it. That just won't happen."

Aroha twisted around in his arms, manoeuvring herself to sit across his lap.

"Promise me," she whispered.

"Aroha, I promise nobody will part us. Don't let the past get to you like this," he soothed, tenderly stroking her cheek.

"Sorry. I just didn't know anyone could behave so horribly."

"Isn't that why we learn? We need to be aware so that we are careful to avoid it. If we were younger this would all be too much."

"It might be too much even now."

"No. You're strong and clever. Just remember it's not happening to you."

"But it feels so real."

He chuckled. "It was real. It just wouldn't happen now."

Holding her close, Gerald's lips warmed hers, offering an anchor to the present.

Hungrily, she kissed back, opening her mouth, lapping his tongue with her own. A groan rumbled out of him.

Aroha's hands raked through his hair. Moving, she sat astride him, grinding her hips, making him groan more.

Still in their white, learning robes, they were also grateful for easy access. Pulling them up and over their heads, they were soon naked. The skin-on-skin contact was tantalising. Aroha traced the outline of Gerald's pectoral muscles with her fingers, making him shudder.

He took hold of her hand, and brought her attention back to his lips, kissing her fully.

Guiding her with his hands, he positioned Aroha so she could take his erection inside her pussy. Slowly, she lowered herself. Bit by bit, she took him in, sliding down his length. His hips bucked, helping her glide up and down. It wasn't enough though.

His back slid down until he was lying flat beneath her. His groans got louder as she rocked backwards and forwards, bringing moans from her own lips.

Steadily, she picked up the pace, building the friction. His hands on her hips supported and encouraged every motion.

Her movements became short and jerky as her muscles clenched. Her head was thrown back as shockwaves shot through her, screams rent from her mouth. The aftershock threw her forwards, collapsing down on his chest.

Gasping and groaning, he thrust for the both of them, lurching into his own climax.

His arms held her as they lay there, recovering, panting.

Aroha, lying by Gerald's side, was almost asleep when the dinner gong sounded. Scrambling up, they righted their appearance and headed to the dining hall together.

Chapter 14

"4th April 2070

Sorry I've been quiet. Not much is happening. I'm so protected here that opportunities to discover anything are rare. And my contacts are on the other side of the compound.

With Becky's help, I knitted a blanket for Akamu, and am starting a pair of booties. Heck, I hope nothing goes wrong. Dear Lord, please let us both live for me to see him make use of these.

All us mums-to-be are encouraged to sit and knit and make. Honestly, women staying home doing crafts. Menfolk out there working. Is this 2070 or 1870? Good grief! But at least it's something to occupy our minds and hands.

My belly is increasing, my ankles are swelling; yep, still pregnant.

As little kicks ricochet off my insides, I'm filled with gratitude. I'm so thankful for new life. Deeksha may be rubbing off on me; she's so positive.

But when surrounded presumably by so much death outside, it's somewhat miraculous to be bringing new life to Earth, to Gaia.

1st May 2070

I am trying to conserve paper. There's no point writing about nothing.

Suffice it to say all of us are progressing well with our pregnancies. Deeksha is close to full term now, I think.

Even though we've been through this before, we're still subjected to antenatal classes. Besides, I think Emma's more than happy to have others there with her.

It's funny how we've grouped. Deeksha and I are the experienced ones, helping Emma and Debbie, the newbies. I suppose you have a natural affinity with people of similar experiences. And there are so many differences, even among us mums-to-be; different places of birth, upbringing, cultures, careers. But it's the similarities we find comforting, like the elusive reassurance we all crave.

16th May 2070

Oh, Deeksha gave birth to the most precious little baby girl yesterday. Her partner was actually brought in for her labour. I'm so happy for them.

Aarushi is so adorable. She has her mother's jet black hair, but pale brown skin and ten tiny fingers and toes.

I had a quick cuddle before leaving the family alone. I don't know how long her partner will be here for, so didn't want to steal their time.

Back in my room, I couldn't help rubbing my own belly.

"It'll soon be your turn," I whispered to Akamu.

25th May 2070

It's been just over a week, but Rob, Deeksha's partner only just went back to his zone this morning. It's been really nice to have male company around here. Deeksha was clearly delighted. Understandably, they kept mostly to themselves for the majority of their treasured time.

Deeksha is putting a brave face on it, but I know her well enough by now to realise when she's hurting. I know she's missing Rob. How could she not? I'll try and see her alone soon to see if there's anything I can do.

30th May 2070

Aarushi is on track to becoming the most spoiled baby in all history. We're fussing around her so much. But we can't help it. She's such a happy little girl, and we're all in 'mother hen' mode. There's so much love in her life; for that, she's lucky.

Even better, she's still with her mum. No child-snatchers here!

5th June
Umm…quick note. I've gone into labour. Ouch!

6th June

Fetu here. Rachel is a bit tired right now, having brought Akamu into the world. She's amazing. He's amazing. I'm a dad!!

Rachel says he looks like me. But I can see her in him too, he scrunches up his little nose just like she does.

Thank the heavens, I'm a dad and am here, able to be present for my wonderful woman and little boy. I have a son!!

7th June

I'm sitting here, giggling like a schoolgirl, having read the last diary entry. I think Fetu's a little bit happy and proud to be a father. And I don't blame him one little bit. Our son is glorious.

It was such a relief when Fetu gave his verbal approval to the name Akamu. His eyes sparkled a little more. He wasn't crying. Big, tough army men don't cry. Unless maybe they've just become a father.

The girls have come in for cuddles, of course. But likewise want to give our little family some privacy, just as we did for Deeksha, Aarushi and Rob.

I'm sore and tired still. My Akamu isn't a small boy and there wasn't a water-bath option. We have the best maternity ward imaginable, but the doctors were still keen on a natural birth. Fetu was by my side, and I must've come close to breaking even his strong hands, despite the gas and air.

It occurs to me there must be a limited supply of things like nitrous oxide. Heck, is there going to come a day when mothers won't have even that when they give birth? Please tell me someone is able to reproduce this stuff. We have some scientists, pharmacologists and manufacturers, right?

15th June

It was a lovely week with Fetu; a respite from anxiety. Our little baby boy is here and happy and has a great pair of lungs on him!

Fetu had to leave us this morning. It seems Sunday is the chosen 'tear a family apart day'. It was awful having to say goodbye, but I'm so thankful for the time we had.

It sounds ridiculous for an independent woman, but I feel so safe when he's with me. Can you blame me? So much here feels threatening.

Before Deeksha gave birth, we didn't even know if we'd be able to keep our babies. We're frog-marched about on military schedules in an alien environment. Who wouldn't feel unnerved?

Maybe after a year I should be used to it. But the truth is, I don't think I'll ever be OK with this harsh existence.

So yeah, Fetu makes me feel safe.

17th June 2070

It seems Emma was feeling left out as she went into early labour yesterday evening. Bless her, there were some complications. It was touch and go for a while, but the excellent medical team can congratulate themselves on a 100% success rate so far.

Welcome Bunker baby, Noah. I thought maybe Emma was going for the guy who rescued animals two by two, but apparently, it was a really popular name in the US. And it means peaceful, rest or long-lived.

It seems we've all given a lot of thought to these names, and we've each selected ones which instil some form of hope. Fetu said that in Samoa, they believe names can have a sway on the person's life, be a little prophetic. Let's hope so. All our new babies will have peaceful, happy lives if that's right.

Emma's partner, Andy, is here now. I'll say it again; it's awful we can't live as families. They make such a wonderful group. We all do. Even the mums who moved in with their children don't have the fathers present. They're presumably off doing busy and important things. Only the single dads are here.

Fetu called this the family zone. I'm sure that's the term the leaders use. It's not. It's the maternal zone. A place to keep the women quietly shut away from the rest of society like we're outcasts. Is this what they're building? Some sort of Stepford life? But I'm allowing my negativity to creep back in. My militancy serves no purpose. There's nowhere for it to go. Deep breaths!

Akamu needs a calm, steady mummy. He needs me alive.

1st July 2070

Akamu fills my days with joy but is keeping me busy. I'd almost forgotten how endless the feed, burp, nappy change, amusement, schedule is. Becky takes over when I really need to sleep, but I'm reluctant to let her do that too often. I'm his mum, I need to do this. And maybe I'm still holding onto the fear that Akamu will be taken away whilst I'm asleep.

Disposable nappies don't exist here. It's back to cotton terry towels for our babies. When I see how many clothes and nappies they get through, I'm aware how much washing is involved; the water used. Maybe the leaders are right not to encourage births yet. Good God, what am I saying? I know we have to be careful of our resources, but I shall not condone their behaviour.

6th July 2070

My little Akamu is one month old. He makes me so proud. Such a good little boy. He's fairly good at sleeping, and often has a beautiful smile for me. When those little eyes sparkle and he beams at me, I'm reminded of his daddy so much that my heart could burst.

I miss Fetu so much. It's ridiculous – it's not like we were together a lot before, but it feels like he should be here with us. Even if we'd had a normal relationship, I would be considered an army wife. And they always had to watch their husbands go off on active service for months if not years at a time. Really, I'm no worse off than any of them ever were. I'm luckier in some ways as I have Becky and the other mums in a specialised environment. The clock's not ticking down on maternity leave – there is no job for me to do here. If anything, Akamu has given me a purpose.

Don't think I've forgotten about my other family. The comparisons come up daily, especially to Joshua, what he was doing at this age etc. I know Deeksha suffers the same. We talk about them, keep their memory alive. But we also have to live. We carry on for our little ones.

1st August 2070

Time is flying by. Akamu seems to enjoy Green Space 2 as much as his mummy does. We have prams to push them around in. The other mums come up and coo over him and Aarushi. They've somehow lowered a barrier between them and us. We're safe to talk to now. It's wonderful having a wider sense of community and friendship.

We may have travelled here from the far corners of Gaia, but we are Bunkerites together. We no longer have a nationality. Our traditions and cultures are slowly mingling. We're all resistant to this, of course. We know what we've been taught, been instructed on and brought up with. But the more we're treated as one perhaps the more we become one.

We mothers are all given the same sort of dresses. It's our new uniform. Hey, it's better than constant scrubs. I'd kill for a comfy pair of trackie bums and a baggy sweatshirt right now though.

The point is, we're all treated the same. Our identity is being eroded. And I can't decide whether that's good or bad. Surely our differences are what make us interesting? But can they not also cause conflict?

There were no Easter celebrations. No festivities at all. Life is a bit bland, really. But we are existing. That's what we need to do. Get on, carry on.

1st September 2070

Our babies are continuing to grow and develop. Akamu is almost three months old already. He's going to grow up big and strong, just like his daddy. The UVB lights in Green Space 2 are supposed to help provide vitamin D and he's being given small doses of supplements too. We don't want anyone getting rickets!

At least the older children are able to run and play in Green Space 2. Looking at them, you'd think they were experiencing a normal childhood.

With so little male influence, I do worry over their balance of opinion/behaviour. It's just not right, is it? But we're doing the best we can.

3rd October 2070

Has it really been a year since I entered this zone? Where did that go?

Life is nothing if not routine.

And whenever I feel down, all I need to do is look at Akamu. He is my joy, my hope, my everything.

1st November 2070

Not much to report still. I don't want to be a mummy bore.

Akamu is amazing, and I could fill whole pages of his every movement, but that's not terribly in keeping with the Diary Directive. It's a struggle to stop myself. There's so much I want to say.

Suffice it to say I'm still breastfeeding. The advice is to do so for two years. Really? But we are told our milk is safer than the other options. Better safe than sorry!

As I tick off the months, it occurs to me I've not described the lack of seasons in my diary. We never feel the chill of winter or the warmth of summer. No storms. No picnics on the beach. No sun, no moon, no stars. I miss the rainy days where we would snuggle up at home with hot drinks and have extra cuddles the most.

The temperature is monotonously constant. Possibly more owing to the underground setting than any fancy, energy-draining air-conditioning. It remains beyond my knowledge how these things are actually run.

A few more expectant mothers have come into our zone. That too has become routine. The poor women are usually frantic, scared out of their wits. And we approach them, letting them know the better parts of our experience.

21st November 2070

Debbie has managed to bring Oliver into the world. It happens to be his father's name. But is so fitting for our tree expert. Named after the olive tree, also a symbol of peace. Yes, we're still wishing peace upon our little ones.

He has his mother's bright blue eyes – so vivid. Just gorgeous.

Obligatory cuddles were issued. Every new life is still a miracle, something to be celebrated in whatever small way we can.

1st December 2070

Welcome to the new Christmas!? It's not actually Christmas, of course.

Yes, the erosion of traditions continues.

A nominal date has been chosen for "Winter Festival". I don't think it will catch on.

It's not celebrating anything. It's a non-offensive date, somewhere close to Diwali, Hannukah and Christmas. It's none of those things. What are we celebrating?

The lighting conditions in here haven't changed. How do we know that it's even winter? For the love of God! But I suppose they're trying, in their characteristically cold-hearted way. It's logical to them.

Personally, I think learning to embrace differences may be more beneficial.

Anyway, this "Winter Festival" means we get so see our partners. Thank you for your generosity, oh mighty leaders!?

Fetu wrapped me up in his strong arms as soon as he saw me. Ah, my pillar of strength! But he quickly turned to Akamu, who's, "Grown so much." The giggles that bubbled from our son were heart-warming as he too experienced that protective embrace; so strong yet loving and gentle.

Having been showered in kisses, we went to our dining hall.

Chickens have been sacrificed, I mean cooked. The same offerings as we had at Christmas last year. It's tasty, so nobody complains. But there's a missed opportunity, isn't there?

Everyone was in good cheer as we ate. And at the end, we got up and sang. In the absence of "Winter Festival" songs, those of each old faith present sang something from their culture. People joined in what they knew and were keen to learn what they didn't.

Enough Kiwis were present to perform a haka, which was delightful if not a little scary. Fetu joined in, my fierce warrior.

Tears fell as we joined hands in a large circle and (those who knew the words) sang Imagine. It's an old song, written by John Lennon. It was created to inspire peace. It didn't work before, but maybe it'll help now.

The lyrics, asking people to imagine there's no country, religion or war – just wow! How much more meaningful those words are now. We're living it, John; no countries or religion. Not quite what you meant, I think. May achieve your dream of peace. Thank you for your words and inspiration.

2nd December 2070

Bliss! Fetu was allowed to stay overnight. Hoorah! Maybe the leaders are starting to appreciate the importance of families?

Of course, Becky was still in the room too, so no shenanigans took place. It was just lovely to have his large, warm body next to mine. I swear Akamu slept better too.

Waking up to that smile? I may be in heaven!

He had to leave at midday. We were told first thing, so had the chance to prepare.

I wish he could stay longer but realise that it would never be enough, not unless it was permanent.

The week we had after Akamu was born was terrific, but that parting was so much harder."

"And there ends another year. That seems to have gone by real quick, Rogno," Gerald commented.

"Well, sure. You notice how there were fewer diary entries in 2070. Why do you think that was?"

"Dr. Rachel said, didn't she? She was busy with a newborn baby and there wasn't much to report. With her hands full, she wasn't able to stickybeak so much," Aroha said.

Rongo laughed. "I'm not sure stickybeak is quite the word I'd use. She was investigating more before. It was kind of important to find out about her surroundings, what may happen. But now she's feeling safer, people are looking after her and she has Akamu to look after."

"He sounds so cute. I wish I could have seen him," Hana chimed.

"Let's do it then. Everyone close your eyes. What do you think Akamu looked like? A little Samoan/English baby with dark hair and brown eyes. Can you see his smile? He was probably quite similar to our own babies."

Some awws sounded around the class.

"Alright, let's get you home to your own parents."

Aroha gave her mum and dad an extra hug when they got home, happy to live with them both. It hadn't occurred to her before the diary that any other situation was possible. This is just how life was. More and more, she was realising the great blessings of her life.

Chapter 15

The next day, Rongo had an announcement to make. "OK, this is an interesting time. At this point, the diary stops. Dr. Rachel was encouraged to write up the progress of her son. She was actually given a book in which to do so, and a reading copy of that is in the library if you want to read it."

Rongo looked at all the confused frowns.

"There has been speculation over the years, that Dr. Rachel was fearful of discovery. That she hid her real diary in an attempt to avoid getting herself or Fetu into trouble. Maybe she was just preoccupied with Akamu. Or she was scheming and avoiding writing anything incriminating. But whatever the reason, she stops writing in this one for a long while."

"Is that it then?" Aroha asked.

"Not quite. We saw in 2070 that Dr. Rachel was suffering a little ennui. The important news was that Akamu was born and they stayed together. He brought happiness into her life. Fetu was allowed occasional visits. Things continued in that vein. She and the group of mums were all looked after, their babies growing as best they could."

"Wait. Is that in the other diary?" Hana asked.

"Yes, the librarian knows who's done this course, so you will have access rights once we're done here. You can read all about the early days of Akamu."

Hana nodded in appreciation.

"OK, so let's pick up four years later when Dr. Rachel starts writing in this diary again…"

"*12th March 2074*

Today marks five years that we've been here. It's been tough, but we've made it. We were all looking forward to finally going outside…

But of course, the leaders have decided it's too cold at the moment. We'd better wait for the summer. The temperatures are still far lower than we're used to even then.

Over time, we have had to come to accept what we've been given. But now anger and resentment are increasing again.

Surely, they knew this before. Why didn't they tell us? It's a bitter blow.

1st April 2074

The atmosphere is thickening. Even amongst us mums, we're anxious to break free. We've been trapped in here for so long. We want out! NOW!

The messages coming through our item positioning system suggest the other zones are worse. Mounting tension is indicated. I'm not sure if that means fights have broken out yet, but I fear they will do soon if they haven't already.

1st May 2074

It seems suspiciously quiet. I'm not sure if the increased vigilance is making the message carriers wary, or if they've somehow been subdued. Previous entries show my fears of this, that there was some sort of sedation taking place.

Along with possible contraception here. Several of us have had stolen moments with our partners on their visits. Given we're in the maternity zone, our partnerships are fertile, yet nobody here has become pregnant a second time. More and more, I suspect we're systematically drugged.

The pregnant mums eat in their rooms. Only once we're mobile postnatal do we join the communal dining hall – it's fairly easy to administer medication to us and not them.

6th June 2074

Today is Akamu's fourth birthday. How I had hoped he could spend it outdoors. He has known nothing but this hole in the ground his entire life. The poor little guy has no idea what he's missing. To feel the sun on your face, the wind in your hair, the rain on your skin. I want so much more for him. He deserves so much more.

Fetu is here, celebrating the special day. He whispered news of riots. He and his team have had to step in a few times. It goes against his morals, but he must remain a soldier. There are too many dangerous consequences for him to behave otherwise. This way everyone stays alive.

And that was before the quieting. He too suspects some form of sedation is in force. We both hope they're careful with doses and there will be no long-term side effects.

It's such a pity. We had found a type of peace here. It wasn't quite contentment, but we had accepted what was in the hopes of gaining freedom.

Akamu ran around Green Space 2 like a maniac after eating some sweet treats for breakfast. Such is his birthday privilege. Fetu chased after him, pretending to be a big scary monster. That, of course, made our son squeal and run faster. At least, he did until he fell over. But Daddy was there to pick him up and dust him off. Then off they zoomed again. They're so good together.

Fetu is a great dad in these all too rare moments. I wish for us all there could be more.

I think we're all hoping to be reunited once we get to the surface. This hope seems futile with no specific origin. Maybe because we see going out as freedom, we're expecting full freedom.

Fetu was allowed to stay long enough to tuck Akamu in for the night. I know there will be tears when his dad's not there to say good morning. Sorry, my boy, you'll just have to rely on your mum again.

1ˢᵗ July 2074

It must be mid-winter out there now. I wonder if there's any chance of an early spring.

How long do nuclear winters last? Five years seems a bit short if you ask me. Not that I'm an expert. A nagging doubt keeps creeping up my spine; maybe we won't get out this year at all.

1ˢᵗ August 2074

Still no new outbreaks of violence have been reported. But the 'you're under close surveillance' warning has gone. We're constantly watched, but sometimes the intensity increases.

We're entering the last month of winter. Perhaps we're all calmer as our hope renews? Calm would be the wrong descriptor. My fingers are itching to grab a door handle and go.

Excitement and anticipation are building. Will we be free by Winter Festival?

1st September 2074

Spring is surely starting. Please, Source, please shine rays down upon Gaia and give us our freedom.

Some of us have started to jog around Green Space 2 whilst the nannies look after the children in the park. We're desperate to run off some of this excess nervous energy.

1st October 2074

Oh, mighty Source, I think I'm going to go stir crazy! Communication remains as poor as ever. One day they may learn that communication is key. Maybe not. If they haven't by now...

I know they said summer. It's not summer yet. Patience. Calm.

Deeksha is as wonderful as ever and keeps taking me through meditations. They help for a while. She says my pitta dosha is my strongest. It feeds my intellectual perception and courage, but also my anger. I'm starting to avoid the fizzy drinks, as that's an artificial stimulant. Perhaps that will help calm me down.

I'm trying my best not to get het up. More than anything, I don't want to negatively impact Akamu. He really takes after his father; so laid back. I don't want to turn him into a stress-ball.

1st November 2074

It's not just me. Even placid Deeksha has started to chew her fingernails. We're on a countdown. Excitement buzzes around every communal space.

When will we be let out? This is whispered like a mantra.

Please don't disappoint us again. There'd be serious trouble, sedative or no, if the leaders don't deliver now.

The children are starting to have more tantrums. I'm sure they're just reacting to our own unsettled emotions. Oops!

29th November 2074

Oh, praise be. Thank you, Source!

We were gathered in our smaller meeting room today. We're going out!!!

Winter Festival, 1st December has been set as our release date. That's in two days!!!

Screams, squeals, shouts all resounded. We cried, hugged and cheered.

Akamu was a bit upset by the commotion. He doesn't understand what's happening. I tried to explain to him but how do you describe a whole world to a boy who knows only a bunker?

Well, I'll just have to show him. A whole new world is literally awaiting him.

I can't begin to describe how excited I am right now! Out! We're going out out!"

"And that's where we have to leave her today," Rongo declared.

"What? No," the class chorused.

Holding her hands up, the reading mistress apologised, "I'm sorry, but trust me, you don't want me to finish after the next entry."

"What? Oh gosh, no, you have to go on," Aroha pleaded.

"And yet I'm not going to. Come on. Let's say our gratitude prayers."

Reluctantly, they closed the session down.

Walking back home, Aroha and Gerald grumbled at each other.

"Why didn't we read on? I'm as anxious as Dr. Rachel must have been. I need to know what happens next," Aroha exclaimed.

"I must admit to being curious. But Rongo must have her reasons."

"I know, but, ohhh…"

"Patience."

"Yeah, yeah, patience. Blah blah blah."

Gerald tickled Aroha, making her cry out as she tried to get away from his devilish hands.

"Stop, stop," she squealed, trying and failing to tickle back.

"Not until you stop complaining."

"Alright, alright, I quit," she said through her laughter.

Gathering her into his arms, Gerald kissed her. Softly at first but deepening as she responded.

"You coming in?" she asked, breaking away.

"No, I have to get home."

"Oh."

He put his hands out. "Don't think I don't want to. I do."

She smiled. "It's OK. I'll see you tomorrow in class."

"Can't wait," he said with a wink before going to his own house.

"30th November 2074

There really isn't much to pack. One of the joys of not really owning anything, I suppose.

We've been told that everything we need will be in our new home. Only sketchy details have been provided, of course. But dwellings are provided on the surface, interlinked by some sort of plexiglass tunnels. It sounds like we'll all be closer, one large community instead of all this separation, but it's possible I misunderstood that. Or it's just wishful thinking.

Nervous excitement reigns supreme all around.

Bring on tomorrow!

2nd December 2074

I apologise to the Diary Directive, but I could not write yesterday for so many reasons. Akamu is now asleep, so can put some words down.

I am not Rachel. This is Nanny Becky. And something terrible has happened.

We were all crammed into trucks like cattle in the Before. The noise was immense.

It was cold still. We had big furry coats supplied which we hugged around us. It was odd when we were given them, but as soon as we were outside, we were grateful for the sunglasses too.

It is not like Before. The sky is grey but bright, even though we could not see the sun. The wind is fierce.

It is barren everywhere you look. Driving along, we saw the abandoned towns and villages. Deserted. I almost expected to see ghosts wandering. Fields are dried and cracked. The stench – it smells like death and dust. Decay.

There is a fuel stop. Trucks have been coming and going for years. They take our waste to our new home where there are biomass facilities. This is what they put in the vehicles. And I think maybe some other things. But they store some here for the long journey too.

It was at this stop that it happened. Fetu was there with another truck, standing guard. Rachel leapt out. I could not stop her. But I did hold onto Akamu and will be forever thankful I did.

The soldiers were edgy all day. She should not have tested them.

She ran to Fetu, crying his name. So excited to see her lover.

They told her to stop. She did not. So, they stopped her. With a bullet, they stopped Rachel.

Down she fell, blood bursting out.

Instantly, screaming, Fetu swivelled and returned fire on the soldier who shot his beloved.

All this time they have waited for each other only to be forever sundered.

Another soldier shot Fetu in turn.

So much blood!

Three bodies lie still on the ground. I had Akamu on my lap, not facing the back of the truck. I held his little head against me, not letting him turn towards the sound of gunfire.

"Go, go, go," the soldiers commanded.

My friends remained on the ground, abandoned. I saw them through my tears, blurred figures. My heart is broken.

What is to become of Akamu? I am responsible for him now. Nobody will take him away. I owe her that much, my brave, foolish friend. She was always so good to me. I will protect him. Rachel, I will keep him safe, I promise."

"What the…?" several people muttered.

"She's dead?"

"What? No."

"That can't be it."

"No, she can't die like that."

So many utterances of disbelief erupted.

People began crying.

"Deep breaths, class. Let me carry on."

"I don't want to hear any more," Hana whimpered, covering her ears.

"You will. Trust me."

"8ᵗʰ December 2074

I am sorry for the subterfuge. We had to be safe, let them think I was dead.

This is Rachel."

Cheers erupted in the class.

Waiting for them to quieten down, Rongo continued.

"What happened?

After a LOT of persuasion, I agreed to the plan. But I would not put Akamu in danger.

I ran to Fetu. His comrade, Sam shot me. Only he didn't, he shot past me. I triggered a blood squib the guys had made and planted in my thankfully large coat.

Fetu then did likewise at Sam.

And another one of their brothers in arms returned the favour for Fetu.

Fortunately, the other soldiers didn't take much convincing that it was better to leave the dead where they were, the following tankers could deal with the bodies. The left pretty damn quickly.

Once they'd gone, we scurried into the small building (I think it was once an actual petrol station and this is where the counter was) and awaited our rescue. One of the waste tankers was making its way back. Three quick blasts of its horn let us know we were safe to break cover. We jumped up into the cab and he took us to a nearby cave.

A local Maori tribe had been hiding and surviving there. The trucker had spotted them one day as he was refuelling. And a plan was hatched.

The poor people! They've been foraging for nuts and berries, eating rats, bats, insects, whatever they could find. They'd managed to raid some local shops in the beginning. The trucker smuggled food to them to help out once he knew they were there. I've no idea how they survived on so little. They're certainly resourceful.

Hopeful of sharing our future home, they were more than happy to help us.

Fetu discovered the leaders weren't even in the bunker. There were a few billionaires who thought they'd do something philanthropic but delegated the handling of it to members of the GFA. The power clearly went to their heads.

We couldn't bear the thought of living the rest of our lives as if we were on some army camp.

When he discovered he wasn't working for the GFA directly, that it wasn't an organised governmental authority in charge, Fetu realised he couldn't go on. Talking to me, he realised civilians shouldn't be treated that way. Not so rigidly, at least. And then when Akamu was born, his protective instinct really took over.

They wouldn't listen to reason. The GFA recruits had taken over and would hear no opposition to their regime. With the well-intentioned billionaires miles away, the special forces asserted full authority. Their way was the only way.

Using a network in the outside quarters, we ambushed the new compound. I won't lie, some people were killed in the campaign. It is deeply regrettable. I had hoped we'd avoid that. Jennifer and Mike were among the casualties. I will mourn them. Spies they may have been, but on some level, they were still friends who had at least given me hope and support. They helped me through those early stages. Without them I may not be here now.

I say we ambushed, but I was at the rear, bringing the non-fighters to the compound once we were given the all-clear.

There was panic and pandemonium at first. Those who'd just lost loved ones in the conflict were taken to a crisis room where counsellors were on standby. Injured were taken to the medical centre.

We gathered the rest in the meeting hall and explained. Our counterparts had been doing a great job of sending word around and keeping "the civilians" as safe as possible, minimising casualties. None of them showed any resistance to the takeover. Once they realised what was really happening, they even cheered.

The forty-two Maori survivors were introduced and welcomed as heroes. I quickly ushered them to the medical unit after the meeting, wanting to see how best to help them. Their hydration levels weren't too bad; there was fresh water in the cave. It had also offered them essential shelter from the eternal winter. But they were malnourished. Mercifully, we have plenty of peanut paste nutrition packs, so we gave them some of those. They will stay in the medical unit until they've regained full health. But their prognosis is good.

We've told everyone to choose their desired accommodation. Any disputes are to be brought to us, the Emergency Council. A better, elected leadership will be put in place once things settle. But for now, we're here to help.

I managed to speak with Becky, to ask her if she'd consider living next door to us. It's her choice, of course.

*And I thanked her profusely for taking care of
Akamu. She eagerly agreed.*

*Ah, my little boy. Being reunited with him after days
of anguish was the best feeling ever. To have his little
arms wrap around my neck as he ran into mine was
pure bliss. I will never ever let him go again, and I
told him so, amongst a plethora of apologies for
having left him at all. Tears ran in rivers down our
cheeks.*

*It's done! We're in control now – we, the people. Our
new life starts here!"*

"Oh my gosh," Aroha and some of her classmates
uttered.

"And so begins our Fort Itude," the reading mistress
announced, her arms held wide.

"She turned badass," Gerald admired.

Rongo chuckled. "She certainly did. Fetu seems to
have been one of the leaders of the rebellion. It is
likely he took her to the Maori to keep her safe more
than with any intention of setting her amidst militant
action. But imagine how much courage it must have
taken them to put themselves in the line of fire. What
if one of the other soldiers had shot first? Any one of
them could have been killed."

"But it was safer than being in the compound?"
Gerald queried.

"The risk was a measured one. And we heard how some people got killed. Dr. Rachel never names anyone except Mike and Jennifer, but there were fatalities on both sides. There were faithful GFA soldiers who had a duty to fulfil. Dr. Rachel tells of chaos and pandemonium in the wake of the campaign, but it must've been worse during."

Joint deep sighs were huffed into the room.

"She left Akamu," Aroha noted.

"Yes. He was almost four years old. It wasn't feasible to subject him to the danger she put herself in. But it must've been agonising for Dr. Rachel. Having lost two children, to be parted in such a way must have taken immense strength of will. But she knew she could trust Becky as Fetu had already managed to get her posted as one of his own team."

"Did he know her Before, do you think?"

"From what we know, they only seem to have met in the bunker. But do you remember the cleaner, Maria, in the medic zone? Later on, in the next diary, we hear how when Fetu was in the SAS, he fought alongside Maria in the Before. She was working undercover as a cleaner in a top hotel when the evacuation took place. The GFA brought her in as a reliable soldier. Fetu helped get her placed so she was in his network."

"Fook me," Gerald exclaimed amidst other astonished utterances.

"All that time. They were so organised, so clever," Aroha admired.

The class discussed their reactions to this latest revelation.

"Honesty, Respect, Fortitude," Rongo called at the session's close.

The class echoed the village motto back, glowing with pride at their ancestor's bravery.

Aroha spoke to her parents that evening, about the extreme action taken by Fetu and his cohorts.

"I don't know if what they did was right. People died."

Her mum replied, "Does there have to be a right or wrong? It happened no matter how we judge it."

"We can't change the past, I suppose. But it just seems so extreme. And yet, they're so celebrated."

"They had been kept cooped up, confined and isolated for five years, sweetheart. You can't judge them through our eyes. Our life is very different. We are listened to, we do practice patience, compassion and acceptance. We have freedom."

"Thanks to Fetu and Dr. Rachel."

"Yes. Rightly or wrongly, they took action against oppression. Maybe the leaders, in time would have become more lenient. But there wasn't really anything in those whole five years that gave them any real hope of that. The precious few concessions they'd gotten were meagre. Fetu was kept away from his own son."

"They were very cruel."

"If you're asking if they deserved to die, of course not. Nobody deserves that. But the rebellion fought for freedom. The very fact that weapons were drawn suggests that the GFA controllers would not have relinquished their tight grip on the community any other way," her father added.

"There had already been so much war and death."

Inviting her daughter closer for a hug as they sat, her mother replied, "Yes, there had. I'm sure they didn't make the decision lightly. It couldn't have been easy. As odd as it seems, they did it for a better future, in the name of peace. It was at least for the right reasons."

"I suppose."

"And we have never experienced anything like it since. That was the last stand. The beginning of peace."

"Strange how such violence led to peace."

"Ironic, certainly. But we remain mindful of all that has passed so we maintain that peace. A great many lessons were learned in the Bunker."

Aroha squeezed her mum tighter, reminding herself of home, safety and love.

Chapter 16

"9th December 2074

This is Fetu. I'm only writing this entry as Rachel's promised never to read it.

I don't want her to know what we had to do. She'd look at me differently. I am/was a soldier. This is what I was trained to do. I don't expect her to understand. Sometimes, difficult decisions must be made.

To minimise casualties, our network had identified the guards and spies who would resist our takeover. At a given signal before the ambush, my teams dispatched their targets as subtly as possible so as not to cause widespread panic.

Whether it was in their beds, when they were on duty, whatever, they were slaughtered. We couldn't take the risk. They would've opened fire. They would've caused ongoing problems, always seeking to regain control.

It's not something I'm proud of. But this is why there weren't more fatalities during the incursion. We killed the few to save the many. Their blood will forever stain my hands and conscience.

As it is, innocents were still caught in the crossfire. It clearly wasn't possible to identify all opposition, but we did our best. Minimised the impact.

I lost friends as well as foe. Their loss is deeply felt. Their sacrifice will not be for nothing.

I pray for their souls and for forgiveness.

I thought it was important to declare this. Rachel has always been open and honest here. So, I've stated the facts for the record.

15th December 2074

A skeleton crew have been at this site all along. It must have been dreadful for them. There's large barns of animals, kept out of the freezing cold. And larger hydroponics labs to grow vegetables. I've seen the biomass plant and solar panel fields. The area is immense.

It's supposedly summer but still cold. Nobody stays outside too long at a time. We quickly discovered the UVA levels are still high despite the chill. But in shifts, they scatter the fields with waste products, trying to add nutrients back in as best they can. Crops haven't been planted yet, it's too soon for that.

Thanks to our network of friends, we know where all the stores are too, so some dried goods and supplies are still available.

All-in-all, we have enough to survive, even with the extra people. Rations will still need to be closely monitored. Some things are unfortunately necessary.

Becky has indeed moved into the hut next to ours. Each little house has a sitting area, two bedrooms and a small kitchenette. There is underfloor heating, powered by the biomass plant. And the walls are thick, so we're nice and cosy.

Home! We have a home now. Not as once was but better than what has been. Fetu, Akamu and me together. Not Theo, Joshua and Ella. And not Liverpool. A new home with a new family.

Emma is overjoyed with the large biodomes. They're very similar to the ones they had at the Eden Project in Cornwall, UK. Some plants, flowers and trees are already being grown in those. But there is a separate large Green Space for communal use. After my visits to the cold, dusty outside, I go there to breathe the clean, fresh air.

Worrying estimates of another fifteen to twenty years are floating around – that's how long it may take for temperatures and the soil to return to normal.

Akamu has an almost permanent look of amazement as he discovers the outdoors and animals. His nose scrunches up at the smell in the barns but he still runs in, happy to pet the cows' or horses noses. The first time a cow mooed at him, he jumped back and landed on his bum. He forgave them very quickly though. He is so inquisitive. He makes me proud every single day.

Fetu has been incredible, helping to organise everyone. Pulling together, we've ensured all the essential tasks are taken care of. Soon, we'll start holding meetings to put better structures in place, ascertain what people feel best suited for.

I want to send the trucks out to seek other survivors. There's a distinct possibility more are out there, and I won't refuse to offer aid any longer.

23rd December 2074

Sam, the former SAS officer who took a bullet with us, has been on the search and rescue team. Sadly, they've not discovered any more survivors yet. They reached a small town, eerie in its empty state.

Perhaps this is too much information, but there were human remains in some of the houses. So, teams of soldiers went and gave them a decent burial, at least.

The food shops and restaurants had been stripped bare. I shudder to think what desperate state those people were in, what they suffered. Even the hardware store's shelves were empty.

The library had been boarded up and secured. Our guys managed to break in and rescue some books. Our own library had mainly dull instruction manual type books. We've now got educational books for the children and some novels for all.

I hope that at least some survivors found food and shelter, discovered safety elsewhere.

25th December 2074

Merry Not-Christmas!

We missed Winter Festival, which everyone seems to think was a stupid idea. But nor is it Christmas today as it once would've been. To be honest, festivities aren't a top priority at the moment.

It is, however, a quieter day. Some part of me felt like marking the day somehow. Fetu and Akamu came with me to the largest biodome. It's not for recreational use, but I wanted to visit the trees in there, maybe connect with a tenuous Christmas symbol.

Paul the hippie was there too. I should probably stop calling him that, but it's what he names himself. He too was drawn to the peace and trees. He apologised for being there! I told him not to be daft, that it wasn't out of bounds totally.

He greeted my family with obvious joy, congratulating us and making a huge fuss of Akamu.

I thanked him for all his assistance over the years. He has agreed to sit on the Emergency Council – his opinion is highly respected.

Taking me to one side, he quietly asked if we truly had freedom now. Edging around the topic, he finally asked if a man could move in with him, if it would cause unrest.

Nobody had known he was gay before. Perhaps that would have precluded him from the Bunker as they were so hellbent on procreating, preserving the so-called best of the species.

Immediately, I wrapped my arms around his neck and kissed his cheek, congratulating him. This brought Fetu closer with a cough, which made me laugh.

"Love is love," my partner commented with a shrug once I'd explained.

"What is freedom when it has limits?" I added.

Fetu, realising how many different cultures we have in our compound, said he'd make sure the patrols monitored Paul's home until everyone displayed acceptance and reassured him that intolerance wasn't an option. It's important to both of us that we embrace all people here. We all have an individual past, but only together do we have a future.

1st January 2075

A new year with a new dawn.

Our peaceful future feels balanced on a knife-edge, as if one false move now may bring down the entire thing.

Now we've seen for ourselves the devastation around us and have attained some level of independence, the past seems to have caught up with us.

Now in a safer environment, communication is open. Free to discuss anything, we all seem to have finally accepted the sickening reality; that the majority of the world is dead. Probably due to a nuclear war.

There is a large hut where we can gather in big groups. We don't all fit at once and it's not feasible to meet outside. It's the best we can do right now. But today, I held a series of remembrance services, along with our inter-faith minister.

We lit a large white candle and offered our own prayers to the fallen; our loved ones and the wider human population. It was solemn and respectful; important. We needed to officially mark their passing in some way, acknowledge what happened.

We also prayed for the safety of the people in the other bunkers. We have no idea how they're coping.

Debbie has invited everyone to a planting ceremony on Sunday, after service, in the floral biodome. One of the horticulturalists here had already been growing a rose in the nursery and it's ready to be transplanted. They proudly announced that it's a Peace rose.

Akamu is making friends. The teachers have formed a makeshift school. Everyone seems to have different ideas on term times though, so it'll take a while for that to be settled. But there are classes and playmates.

Sometimes, it all feels overwhelming, what we're trying to do here. But then Fetu wraps me in those big arms and my fear melts away. I'm not doing this alone. He's here. And we have a committee. One day at a time, we'll build something good together.

We have freedom. We have hope. We have a future."

"So much work lay ahead of them," Aroha murmured.

"They were almost literally starting from scratch. It must have been daunting," Rongo agreed.

"Where would you even start?" Hana asked.

"With the basics. Fortunately, as Dr. Rachel said, there were already people working here. Others joined them, according to their experience. Slowly, gradually, they built from there. Once the essentials were in place they could expand. What's important is that everyone was involved. They started the weekly meetings. Representatives from each section attended, taking forward views from their counterparts. Not that they didn't have their challenges. With so many different cultures and viewpoints, things could get pretty heated. But they worked through their differences. Eventually."

"Order through chaos," Gerald mumbled.

"Sorry, what was that?" Rongo queried.

Gerald repeated what he'd said, a little louder.

"Yes, I suppose it was."

"I didn't realise it was like that," he said, wincing.

"None of her story is pretty. That's why we have to wait until we can process it. But our society didn't just magically happen. It took work and sacrifice as well as love. With tremendous effort, our community was created. The amount of dedication was extraordinary. And it is that we should be thankful for."

"We thank them for their sacrifice," many chanted.

"That's where this diary ends."

Groans echoed around the room.

"But already we've seen how and why Fort Itude was created. Even the name was voted on. If you choose to go on and study the other diaries, you'll see the election process form. Dr. Rachel and her council had originally named it Fort Freedom but word got around about her diary and she allowed others to read it. They soon picked up on her opening wishes of **Honesty, Respect, Fortitude** which resonated so deeply they made it the village motto, and even adopted the last word as a name, lest we forget. And incorporated it in our precious symbol."

"There are more diaries?" Hana asked.

"Of course, but this is the only compulsory one. It contains the most important information we need to bear in mind. You can either sit courses or read the copies in the library."

Murmurs of appreciation and acknowledgement rumbled.

"But for now, this is it."

The class discussed their thoughts and feelings, reflecting on the tragic history laid bare.

Once ready, Rongo announced, "Let us give our thanks to the ancestors."

"Thanks be to them," was echoed around the room by the near-adults.

"May we live by their wisdom," Rongo chanted.

"May we honour them."

"And may we cherish our beloved planet, Gaia."

Bowing forwards, their hands on the floor, the attendants intoned, "Love to Gaia."

"May we always live honestly, respect ourselves, each other and Gaia. And should hard times descend, may we face them with the fortitude of the ancestors."

"Honesty, Respect, Fortitude."

"Thanks be to Source. May we always live in love and grace."

"Thanks be. Love and grace."

As they all sat upright, they observed meditative silence for a few minutes.

On the wooden rest in front of Rongo, she closed the book with a rabbit on the cover, a heart on its nose. And blew out the white candle in its jar.

"You seem disappointed," Aroha said as she walked home with Gerald.

"I am. I guess...no, it's stupid."

"You had a vision that everything was all OK once they broke free?"

He frowned as if pained but nodded.

"So did I," Aroha admitted, glancing down.

"You did?"

Her head snapped back to him. Holding his gaze, she said, "Yeah. It sounds silly now. I mean, of course, it wasn't. Life isn't a fairy tale. It doesn't work that way. I don't know, maybe it's just what I wanted for them."

"It's not like they didn't get their happy ending." His gaze turned softer.

"They were together as a family."

"They had each other." Dipping his head, he tenderly kissed her.

Drawing breath, she asked, "Do you want to come in?"

"Yeah," was his breathy reply.

Their lovemaking was slow and gentle. Affection flowed in every breath and movement. Ripples of respect ran through them as their bodies united. Trails of kisses marked their love. It was as though their two souls became one as they climaxed.

241

They held each other close afterwards, not ready to relinquish their connection, dozing off wrapped in their own world.

"So, what happens now?" Aroha asked as they woke up.

"Now we live," Gerald replied, his voice hoarse with sleep.

His lips brushed hers. "Now we live," he repeated.

They went to dinner together, hand-in-hand. Aroha beamed as they walked in. So many happy people, eating together. They had food, they had shelter and they had love. Most importantly, they had freedom and community; so much to be thankful for.

Epilogue

Aroha began her medical training the next week. She'd already been taught the basics and had seen her mother's work when accompanying her on rounds. It was a great grounding.

On her first day, Aroha's parents offered a present.

"But isn't this your bag, Mum?" she asked, brows scrunching at the slightly tatty medical bag.

"I was merely a custodian. This bag has been handed down through the generations."

Aroha's mouth gaped. "You don't mean..?"

"Yes, this once belonged to Dr. Rachel Rose herself."

Tears streamed down her cheeks. "Oh my gosh."

"She'd be so proud of you, just as I am," her mum said, crying too.

Her father wrapped his arms around both women. "She'd be proud of you both."

Ending the hug, Aroha examined the bag more closely. "I can't believe it."

Her mum laughed. "It can't be that much of a surprise. You knew you're a direct descendant."

"Well, yeah, but I had no idea that her very bag was right here."

"It didn't seem fair to put that kind of pressure on you. You had to be free to make your own choice. But now you have, this bag belongs to you. Take good care of it."

"I'm scared of ruining it. Can't we just keep it at home? Maybe get a new one made?"

Again, her mum chuckled. "I had the very same reaction. But this kind of bag was made to be used. If it finally falls apart, well, so be it. But our family will continue to use it until then."

"But it was hers."

"She being Dr. Rachel. And she wasn't a goddess, Aroha. Dr. Rachel was a very brave, courageous woman but a woman nonetheless. First and foremost, she was a doctor."

"I don't know what to say...thank you," she stammered, kissing her mum.

"OK, now go to class before you're late."

Gerald began his own studies, training to become a teacher. Whilst Hana started her nanny internship.

Generations tended to follow in the footsteps of their families, but they certainly didn't have to. Gerald was the first teacher in his line; his mum was a vet and his dad was a farmer, for example.

All villagers were expected to help out with various basic tasks – menial labour was shared so nobody felt demeaned.

Aroha spent as much time with Gerald as their studies allowed, their relationship solidifying as it grew roots and bloomed.

Armed with the full knowledge of their past, they took tentative steps into the future.

Thank you for reading Love Gaia ~ The Diary Directive.

Please do leave a review, they are more valuable to me than you can imagine and help other readers make an informed decision about whether to make their purchase.

About the Author

TL Clark is a best-selling, award0winning, British author who stumbles through life as if it were a gauntlet of catastrophes.

Rather than playing the victim she uses these unfortunate events to fuel her passion for writing, for reaching out to help others.

Her dream is to buy a farmhouse, so she can run a retreat for those who are feeling frazzled by the stresses of the modern world, and to rescue horses. She is a Reiki master and a bit of a hippie herself, but not quite as much as Paul in this book.

Her writing mission, which she has chosen to accept, is to explore love in its many different and intriguing forms.

Her loving husband and very spoiled cat have proven to her that true love really does exist.

Writing has shown her that coffee may well be the source of life.

If you would like to follow TL or just drop in for a chat online, you can do so on Facebook, Instagram, Twitter, Pinterest, BookBub, YouTube or Goodreads.

@tlclarkauthor will find her on most social media

She also has a blog where she shares random thoughts and book reviews. She's very kind and supportive, so often reviews other indie authors as well as offering writing tips.

www./tlclarkauthor.blogspot.co.uk/

You can **sign up for her newsletter on her blog,** to ensure you don't miss any exciting news (about new releases and special offers). Sneaky peakies are usually shared before other readers get a chance to see the latest book release.

Other books by TL Clark

Young's Love – Striving for independence and finding gelato in Tuscany.

A journey which explores Samantha's cry for freedom. She has an unhappy, controlled marriage that just keeps getting worse.

At breaking point, she goes on a couples' holiday to Tuscany. As she finds independence can she also find love? Can she become the woman she always wanted to be?

Trues Love – Suspense and suspended reality in Ibiza.

Amanda Trueman loves her single, wild and carefree lifestyle. Read about her erotic adventures in this rollercoaster of a book.

She heads off with her best friend to the sunny skies of Ibiza for a holiday which promises to supply even more fun memories.

A blonde bombshell certainly fits the bill, but he soon has her heart exposed as well as her flesh.

Feeling vulnerable, will Amanda sink or swim in the world of true love? Danger lurks. Is their relationship doomed to end in disaster?

<u>Dark Love</u> – A romance novel with BDSM in it too.

This book follows Jonathan, a male Submissive. His attention is grabbed by another woman, but can he bear to turn his back on the life he's always known and loved? Is it even possible?

This book investigates the love that exists in a BDSM relationship and beyond.

<u>Broken & Damaged Love</u> – a book with an important message.

This one comes with a trigger warning, as it features a sexually abused girl.

It was written to give hope to CSA survivors. They too can go on to have healthy, happy relationships.

It also aims to help others watch out for signs, so they can help stop abuse.

Profits are regularly donated to charity from the sale of this book.

<u>Rekindled Love</u> – Hatches, matches and dispatches.

We join Sophie just in time for her first 'experience', but she gets torn away from her first love.

We go on to follow her life, through marriage, birth and death. Hers is not an easy life but hold her hand through the bumpy bits to get to the good times.

There's a rollercoaster of emotions waiting for you.

<u>The Darkness & Light Duology</u> – formed by Love Bites & Love Bites Harder

The paranormal romance

Shakira didn't fit in. The reason why is tragic…the solution is unbelievable.

A rich tale of witchcraft, sorcery, elinefae and a dragon.

Shakira struggles to balance darkness and light.

<u>Self Love</u> – the importance of being kind to yourself

Molly is a self-deprecating florist, at least until The Incident forces her to look at herself differently. Internet dating features with varying results. As does a beautiful friendship.

Full of British humour as Molly discovers the path to personal growth is no bed of roses.

<u>Regency Love</u> – <u>Reflections of a Young Lady</u>

This is the historical romance. Join Lady Anne as she enters the marriage mart. Experience the highs and lows of 1814 through her eyes.

Not all of the Ton are honourable. And not all marriages are equal.

Giving a voice to women who had none at the time.

That's it for now. Don't forget to write that review. Happy reading.

Love and light,

TL Clark